THE MUSIC NEVER DIED

Summertime Jews
H_2O
Instant Karma

The Music Never Died
Tales from the Flipside

MARK SWARTZ

ILLUSTRATIONS BY
JEB LOY NICHOLS

VERSE CHORUS PRESS

Cover and book design by Steve Connell | *steveconnell.net*

Library of Congress Cataloging-in-Publication Data

Names: Swartz, Mark, author. | Nichols, Jeb Loy, illustrator.
Title: The music never died : tales from the flipside / Mark Swartz ;
   illustrations by Jeb Loy Nichols.
Description: Portland, OR : Verse Chorus Press, 2024. | Summary: "Sixteen
   stories that riff on rock and rap mythology to envisage alternate paths
   for music legends who died young"-- Provided by publisher.
Identifiers: LCCN 2024009299 (print) | LCCN 2024009300 (ebook) | ISBN
   9781959163053 (trade paperback) | ISBN 9781959163060 (epub)
Subjects: LCGFT: Short stories.
Classification: LCC PS3619.W37 M87 2024 (print) | LCC PS3619.W37 (ebook)
   | DDC 813/.6--dc23/eng/20240419
LC record available at https://lccn.loc.gov/2024009299
LC ebook record available at https://lccn.loc.gov/2024009300

*Dedicated to musicians everywhere,
but especially to my favorite
singer-songwriter, Jennie Guilfoyle*

These stories contain many verifiable facts and situations but frequently depart from reality in the interests of fiction. The fictional versions of the artists depicted here say and do things that do not always accord with the known words and actions of their real-life counterparts. Many of the songs and recordings described here exist only in these pages. Quotations from actual sources are referenced in the endnotes.

CONTENTS

"*To live past the end of your myth is a perilous thing.*"
—Anne Carson

"*Life, Rowena, is a song. By that I mean it's short, like a song. It's got an unhappy ending, like a song. It repeats itself, like a song. It can be loused up, like a song. You can go reggae or you can go heavy metal. You want fiddles I'll give you fiddles. You want synthesizer I'll give you synthesizer. You want to hear sandpaper, I got guys that can sandpaper your heart into little pieces. So I ask you, is life not a song? Essentially?*"

—Donald Barthelme

"*When someone dies young, everything comes to look like an omen.*"
—Lucy Sante

THE MUSIC NEVER DIED

LIVE FROM AMELIA'S LOUNGE

For Alan Lightman

LIVE FROM AMELIA'S LOUNGE

The velvet curtains part to reveal a baby-faced man in a pin-striped suit brandishing the receiver of a princess telephone.

> *Hel-lo ba-aby! Yeah, this is the Big Bopper speaking.*
> [pause] *Oh, baby, you kno-whoa what I like!*

The audience cheers dutifully at the catchphrase, and they will dance and clap when Ritchie Valens plays, though the main attractions tonight and every night at Amelia's Lounge are still to come. But even in this bastion of stability, times and tastes can and do change. A recent development has shaken up the routine, arousing new and dangerous passions the way only a great pop song can.

> *First, the bad news, in case you haven't guessed already. If you're enjoying the show here at Amelia's this evening, then your flight did* not *arrive safely at its destination. You went up in the air, but you didn't come back down. Well, your body did, in one state or another, after a sudden loss of cabin pressure and*

an abrupt drop in altitude, followed by an even more abrupt deceleration, but your soul—along with the clothes you were wearing—remains here on a different kind of plane . . . the Astral Plane.

Every religion gets it wrong. It's not about going up to heaven or down to hell depending on whether you were good or bad. There's no underworld or happy hunting ground, no Valhalla where all the dead folks gather.

It's much better organized than that. It's all determined by cause of death. The suicides stay together; the murder victims are somewhere else. If you're felled by a heart attack, you're assigned to one place, a stroke and you go to a different place. Air-crash fatalities permanently reside on what the Big Bopper calls the Astral Plane. (In case you're wondering, the kamikazes are grouped with the suicides.)

I personally can't think of a better or more cultured crowd of folks with whom to spend eternity, so maybe it's not such bad news after all. And the really good news is that the music here can't be beat. What's more, the cocktails are on the house. At Amelia's, we like to say, all you need is an ear and a heart.

A little history: When Amelia Earhart founded this establishment in 1937, she wanted it to be a haven for all who found themselves in her predicament—which, back in those days, was still quite novel. The club was classy and intimate, but there was no music to speak of at first. That all changed in 1944 when Glenn Miller showed up. A tireless, unstoppable showman, he made the afterlife entertaining, and not just with his trombone; his liaison with movie star Carole Lombard became the first celebrity romance in this growing metropolis. Amelia's put up a bandstand, put down a dance floor, and from that point on the joint was jumping.

Three newcomers arrived on February 3, 1959, and big band music almost immediately fell out of fashion. Buddy Holly, Ritchie Valens, and J.P. Richardson Jr (known as the Big Bopper) tore the place up night after night, entertaining people from all over the world. Holly performed not only his own hits but also chart toppers he learned from fans who turned up over the years.

> *Glenn and his band still perform from time to time, and evidently things can get pretty peppy. I mean it—don't miss out on the chance to catch a trombone legend. I'm told the Early Bird Special is quite a treat.*

For the next eight years, rock and roll dominated Amelia's Lounge. There was no real competition to speak of. Patsy Cline caused a stir when she appeared in 1963, but it was nothing compared to the explosive debut of Otis Redding and the Bar-Kays at the end of 1967, after their aircraft plunged into an icy Wisconsin lake. They played with relentless, precise timing but also improvised with abandon, startling audiences each night with new arrangements, surprise tunes from the past, and inexhaustible jams of incredible virtuosity. Their orgiastic version of "Pennsylvania 6-5000" brought about an unintentional kerfuffle with Glenn Miller, and they respectfully retired the number thereafter.

Having seen Miller wilt, Holly was determined not to follow him into obsolescence. He studied Redding, brushed up on his Robert Johnson, Bob Wills, and Louis Jordan, and forced the band to rehearse three hours a day. Somehow he got ahold of Beatles and Stones records, and he mastered new moves, new chords, new rhythms.

Redding laughed off the competition at first, but quickly realized that putting Holly out to pasture wasn't going to be all that simple. Both acts got better and tighter, and every year brought fresh planeloads of music fans to Amelia's to catch an incredible twin-headliner bill. Some nights Holly went on first; some nights Redding did. They constantly outdid each other, and the music reached new heights, so to speak.

Over the years, Amelia's welcomed new stars to the stage—Ronnie van Zant and Steve Gaines from Lynyrd Skynyrd (you can guess their most requested song), John Denver, Stevie Ray Vaughan—but the balance of power held all the way up until August 25, 2001, when Aaliyah walked into the club and took hold of the microphone.

You people are looking especially beautiful tonight, and that's why I'm especially pleased to welcome Señor La Bamba himself, Ritchie Valens!

Trauma having awakened his ethnic pride, Valens does a thrilling all-mariachi set. He delivers an extended bilingual monologue on why Mexico is entitled to reclaim Texas. This may just be to razz Holly's home state a little, but it is the only political content to be found at Amelia's. The other performers have lost interest in earthly power struggles.

Ritchie and I are good. We are damn good, and handsome too, but the man about to step onto these illustrious floorboards—what can I say, he's Mozart, Beethoven, and Muhammad Ali rolled into one. Ladies and gentlemen, the Zeus of rock and roll, Charles Hardin "Buddy" Holly!

Opening with a bracing "That'll Be the Day"—which takes on a new if obvious irony on the Astral Plane—Buddy Holly and the Crickets blaze through his own discography alongside new spins on the Who's "Substitute" and the Kinks' "You Really Got Me," among others. The bespectacled dervish reclaims punk from the punks, spraying loud fast originals that wouldn't sound out of place on a Ramones or Cramps album. His showstopper is a drawn-out, trickily syncopated rendition of the hit that elevated him to the status of secular saint, Don McLean's "American Pie."

Oh, baby, you kno-ow what I like! Did I just have a heart attack or what? Ladies and gentlemen, take this chance to catch your breath and tie your shoe-laces because we're just getting started. Let's have another round of applause for His Royal Majesty Buddy Holly, that's right. And now it is my honor and pleasure to introduce, all the way from Macon, Georgia, the second coming of the soul lord, Otis Ray Redding, Jr!

The Bar-Kays burst out of the gate with two added key-boardists and a second drummer muscling up the sound of "Hard to Handle." A sweating Redding addresses the crowd: "This is a song Barry Gibb of the Bee Gees wrote for me, that I didn't have time to record before I punched my ticket." He throws his arms out wide, miming a plane heading for a crash landing, and "To Love Somebody," complete with Funkadelic-style chants and Prince-like heavy breathing, fills Amelia's with an unearthly groove. After a medley of disco hits—"I Will Survive," "Stayin' Alive," "Shake Your Body (Down to the Ground)"—he dismisses his band to belt out an a cappella "Dock of the Bay," which segues into "Amazing Grace."

Hel-lo ba-aby! I do believe I sprained some kind of muscle in my groin! Lord have mercy, ladies and gen-tlemen, but you just witnessed the apotheosis of soul. Otis Redding! Let's give him a round of applause! But wait ... Did you think we were done? Did you imagine it was time to go home? Well, I very much beg to differ.

Holly and Redding shared something besides prodigious talent. Understand, mores on the Astral Plane are somewhat more elastic and forgiving than on Earth. If you thought *Life is short* justified permissiveness, you can probably guess what *We're going to be here forever* does to men with an Olympian predilection for philandering. The two men's rivalry went beyond the stage and into the boudoir. They would chase the same flight attendants. If one started dating a fashion model, the other would find one who was even more stunning. If one started dating an heiress, the other would find one who had been even wealthier.

Aaliyah had grown accustomed to older men thinking they could control her and through hard experience had developed strategies for making them think they were pulling the strings, when in fact she retained full self-sovereignty. Behind downcast eyes and shy smiles, she would outwork and outwit any would-be Svengali.

Holly invited her to sing backup on "It Doesn't Matter Anymore" and had her return the night after that. Backing vocals morphed into duet vocals, and soon she had a showcase, wowing the crowd with her gospel-infused "Not Fade Away." Redding, too, caught wind of the newcomer and brought her onstage to play the Carla Thomas part in "Tramp." In his set, too, she had a solo moment in the spotlight with her sultry take on "Try a Little Tenderness."

Both men wanted Aaliyah in their acts and in their beds, but this woman—barely out of girlhood, fresh from Bahamian calamity—resisted their charms. More than that, she brought them to heel. She made them roll over and beg. It was a remarkable display, all the more so because she wielded her power so softly.

Ladies and Gentlemen, it is my distinct privilege to announce a historic headlining debut, by one of the brightest stars to ever blaze across Amelia's stage, the one and only Aaliyah!

Shrouded in darkness, the backing band plays a slinky vamp until the spotlight finds a beauty in a tight ruby-red gown. She steps up to the microphone, her posture relaxed and unapologetic, and sings "One in a Million," from her album of the same name. The crowd shows appreciation but remains seated.

We're going to talk about the sperm and the egg. Y'all okay with that? I just got here, so I wouldn't know for sure, but it seems to me that sperm and egg don't really matter much anymore. Up here, they can't do what they were made to do.

One in a million. When Missy and Tim wrote that song for me, I thought a million was a big number. A million dollars. A million people. A million miles! That's a long way to go, right? But think about it: All of us have been going around the sun once a year, so we've traveled a billion miles or more.

Sperm and egg, honey. When your mom and dad made love, there were seventy trillion different combinations of DNA they could have passed on to you. You and I came into existence against astronomical odds. And let's not even pretend to try and factor in the mind-bogglingly unlikely chain of events that led to space junk and sunlight interacting in the exact way needed to produce and sustain life.

How much of humankind has ever gotten to fly? One percent? Less? Our ancestors never left the earth. For nearly all of human history, flight belonged to birds and bugs. You and me, we flew, baby. We rose higher and higher, and in a way, we never came down.

Doubly blessed by the miracles of life and flight,
how can I keep from singing?

Aaliyah repeats the last six words, fitting them into a
melody she learned from an Enya album, but which dates
back to a nineteenth-century hymnal. Here at Amelia's tonight for the very first time, three planeloads of passengers,
though still stunned by their recent fate, sway to the music as
the band cushions her voice with flute, maracas, and double
bass. The pace picks up song by song as she hits the high-
lights of her all-too-slender catalog.

We're space dust, you and me, but we still feel pain,
right? We still bruise when somebody slaps our face.
We still cry out when they step on our toes. We still
feel the sting when they try to rob us of our dignity.
That's what somebody did to me. I'm not going to
say his name. I'm not giving him any kind of credit
or recognition for what he did when I was just a
young, innocent child. What I'm going to do, and I
want you all to help me, is I'm going to take something from him—to get back at him for taking something from me. This man, this monster, somehow he
was blessed with song. At least one magical song, but
after tonight, if you all help me, that song won't be
his anymore. It will be ours.

Buddy Holly and Otis Redding join Aaliyah Dana
Haughton at the microphone. The titans have never before
shared a stage. A hush falls over the crowd as the band eases
into an elegant shuffle.

Redding offers a line about feeling sometimes like you
can't go on. To which Holly responds by crooning how
life often seems like merely a bad song. And then the three

singers lean into the microphone together: "I believe I can fly, I believe I can touch the sky," while every member of the audience, bathed in blue light, stretches out their arms and exuberantly joins the chorus.

LOOK MA NO LIVER

"My name is my name."
—Marlo Stanfield

"Seeing is forgetting the name of the thing one sees."
—Robert Irwin

LOOK MA NO LIVER

The first blast shattered the window, and he caught a glimpse of the shooter's crayon-yellow bug-eyed face.

"Why you wanna do that?"

"Now who's the rhyme assassin?"

The next three bullets bit the rapper's shoulder, hip, and thigh. He heard the next shot over the shouts of the driver and other passengers, so he knew it wouldn't kill him. He would not die in the passenger seat of a GMC Suburban, after leaving an awards ceremony, at the hands of a man wearing a Bart Simpson mask.

The last bullet punctured a lung but missed the liver and heart by millimeters, and the assailant escaped into the Los Angeles night. It took the paramedics close to an hour to extract the 380-pound star from the vehicle. He lost gallons of blood but he survived. In a later freestyle he recalled, "Forgiven? Me? / The Jaws of Life delivered me / This n—be / At liberty / Incidentally / I'm liver free."

Cedars-Sinai Medical Center refused to confirm that he was a patient. They allowed his mother, Voletta, to visit on the condition she follow strict orders for evading attention. She managed to smuggle in butter crunch cookies and Pringles to her son, which he ate while she read him get-well messages from fans and friends. He glumly tolerated her repeated invocations of Jehovah to "sustain him on his sickbed."

✖

It was all a dream. The first five words of the most important hip-hop track of all time. Is he merely referring to his youthful aspirations as a rapper, or do the words encompass everything in his life up until that point? Everything in the universe? It was *all* a dream. Now, he implies, the dream is over. A new world begins.

After three weeks the doctors granted permission for the rapper to be transferred to Hidden Pond, the gated community on Long Island where Voletta lived in a large, recently constructed home with French doors and a four-pillared portico. A hospital bed and round-the-clock medical care were arranged.

Because the incident came just six months after the fatal shooting of the rapper's one-time friend and recent rival, a tidal wave of media attention ensued, but the curtains remained shut and interview requests went unanswered. Hoodied figures heaving gym bags came and went without acknowledging the cameras.

Stories proliferated as his recuperation stretched on. Speculation that he had died competed with rumors that he was hiding out on an estate in Jamaica. A vociferous contingent of the conspiracy-minded hip-hop community placed him in Sing Sing Correctional Facility, where FBI interrogators were keeping him on life support for various twisted purposes. Tabloids printed manipulated photographs of a look-alike languishing on a rickety cot.

Eventually the frenzy subsided and Voletta's insistence on privacy was respected. If watchers of her Long Island home had stuck around until a sunny afternoon in early May, however, they would have observed a chocolate-brown limousine sliding down the street and into the driveway.

✖

"You want some juice?" Voletta asked.

He pantomimed chopsticks and a bowl.

"You finished that last night, remember?"

He rubbed his belly.

"I'll order some more then."

He pushed two invisible cylinders toward his mouth.

"And egg rolls. Of course, egg rolls."

Lungs are a rapper's instrument. It takes considerable wind power to force air into percussive, concussive syllables that explode on contact with the mic. In his prime, he had lacked the vocabulary and, perhaps, the lyrical agility of his compeers, but in a rap battle he could blow your house down. Even Chuck D. sounded puny set against him.

In his leopard-skin bathrobe, he blended into the leopard-skin couch. His girth had returned, but he was barely communicative, watching kung fu movies and wildlife documentaries with the TV on mute. He would flip listlessly through his mother's bible and dog-ear the pages over her mild objections. He taught his surprisingly nimble fingers to make origami cranes.

His instrument had suffered major damage, and any effort at speech felt pointless if it couldn't rattle the walls. He told Voletta he trusted the silence. He wrote this assertion on a square of origami paper.

She said trust was dangerous.

What does that mean? he wrote.

"Trust is what gets a person killed," she sighed.

You think that's what happened? He scrawled. *You think I was ~~killed~~ shot by someone I trusted?*

✖

Voletta enlisted a voice coach, who recommended an ear, nose, and throat specialist, who placed a call to an Upper East Side pulmonologist. Dr. Ruben came on a biweekly basis, putting the star through a series of tests and leaving instructions for exercises to be rigorously followed between visits.

"You want to rap again, don't you?"

He shrugged his massive shoulders. Dr. Ruben instructed him to inhale and exhale five times quickly. He had him blow just hard enough into a long plastic tube to keep a red piston suspended between two hash marks, no harder.

Voletta said the doctors in Los Angeles had given her son too much "weak blood." The doctor scowled and offered to refer the patient to a psychiatrist.

Gradually, the rapper began to speak, in a halting, muffled way, and almost against his will the syllables at the end of his sentences started to rhyme. The chocolate-brown limousine would arrive from time to time, disgorging a purposeful man in tailored clothes who would stay a few hours, watching videos with his investment and complimenting Voletta's cooking. The impresario never removed his shoes or his shades, which had all been tinted to match his exact skin tone.

"We have got to solve this mother," he said, gazing down at his wingtips with their 24-karat eyelets and aglets.

"Yeah?"

"Yeah. We need to figure out who did this to you."

"I don't want to talk to the cops."

"Cops?" he spat. "The cops can fuck their cop dogs atop a mile-high pyramid of bullshit, but *I* know people who can conduct a thorough investigation with guaranteed results."

"I don't know."

"That's cool. You keep your weight up and let your body heal itself. Let them that love you, love you."

"Maybe we shouldn't have released 'Who Shot Ya?'" the star said, referring to the track that had made light of a violent attack on his nemesis—who had duly responded with "Hit

'Em Up," perhaps the most wrathful rap ever recorded. "We had a lot of other jams."

"You think he did this? Like from the grave?"

"Revenge is a dish best served cold."

"Not *that* cold." On the screen a school of zebrafish swirled in enormous fractals.

"We don't want more trouble."

"It's no *trouble*," the impresario replied, his voice breaking. "It's what family does."

Neither had a dad growing up. Both had made large fortunes quickly. Both had run afoul of the law and ex-girlfriends and seen friends die too soon. They had lost count of the number of tracks they'd cut together, back when the rhymes used to gush like Niagara and nobody had to get clearance for the samples.

Their fortunes were entwined. It would be wrong to say the rapper had secured the executive's clout, just as wrong as it would be to say that the impresario had singlehandedly engineered the rapper's ascent. But their connection was deep and strong, like that of separated but formerly conjoined twins.

✖

Voletta mistrusted the impresario, but she knew the comeback was inevitable. Still, what was the rush? The bullets were still hot. Those shots had been fired only two and a half months earlier, and burly men were already pushing canvas-draped recording equipment up a ramp and installing a 10,000-watt generator to power it.

Speculative interview requests continued to arrive, and a writer from *S.P.I.T.* magazine (Special People's Intelligent Talk) who had cultivated a long friendship with the rapper got the nod. Voletta remembered her manners and the small gold cross at her throat. The impresario said that she would play ball, whatever that meant.

Latitia van Eyck arrived on a powder-blue Vespa. No helmet. Five feet tall in high-heeled black boots that squeaked when she walked.

"Who did it?" she asked, brushing a dreadlock aside to reveal a hazel eye.

He shrugged. "Someone who wanted me dead, I bet."

"What's so great about dying?" she said, a pointed reference to his albums *Ready to Die* and *Life after Death,* whose titles implied a longstanding death wish. "Everybody does it, sooner or later."

"Not all of them have the guts to look death in the eye, though." He hadn't told anybody the shooter was wearing a Bart Simpson mask. That just wasn't gangster.

"You're not scared?" she challenged. "Tell me you weren't scared when that guy pointed his gun at you."

"I lived to tell the tale," rapper said.

"Then *tell* it."

"I think death might be kind of scared of *me*, now that you mention it," he winked.

"*That's* what you think?"

"Yeah, little baby death shit his pants probably, see. Death better take out a life insurance policy."

The reporter raised an eyebrow at the off-rhyme in his bravado. "This is attempted murder." She wanted a story from the rap legend, but she also wanted to disrupt his recklessness. Even in the presence of his mother, she felt the need to mother him. "Are the authorities investigating?

"If they are, nobody told me about it."

"What would you tell them if they asked you?"

"Not to waste their time. Listen, could you go get me a bucket of fried shrimp, Tish? We ordered some, but when it finally came that shit was cold as shit."

Nobody but him called her Tish. She remembered the time he freestyled for her in the back of a tour bus, rhyming it with *puffer fish, stylish, Coleridge,* and *eat the rich.*

"You don't even want to find him."

"What difference would it make?"

"Justice would get served."

"What's that mean?"

"Don't you want to take an evil man off the street?"

He pondered the suggestion. "N—— probably didn't even *want* to do it. Somebody made him, probably. Tricked him."

"Then don't you want to get the one who tricked him?"

"Yeah, but somebody might have tricked *him*, too."

She asked how far away the shrimp place was, and he gave her fifty bucks.

Van Eyck's interview was the only one he gave. It concluded: "Everyone, it seems, has a theory, except the universally beloved Goliath who caught the lead."

✖

The impresario was furious that the article failed to tease the new album. He'd invited an A-list from the hip-hop world and beyond to the launch, including a Grammy-winning classical pianist (the French doors had to be removed to accommodate his Steinway), a Broadway institution, and a hefty hardcore guitarist whose gyrations threatened to topple Voletta's glassware. The pulmonologist posted no-smoking signs and ordered three different types of air purifiers. The headliner chomped on chocolate cigars and taught his guests how to fold paper birds.

Voletta served oxtail soup and guava juice. She took an immediate shine to the theater legend, who was unfailingly tender with the recuperating star, and she didn't even mind the flailing guitarist, but she didn't know what to make of the slight, elderly Japanese woman dressed entirely in black.

"Can you put that cigarette out, please?"

"Yes of course," she replied, taking one last drag.

"Absolutely no smoking in here, Miss . . ."

"I am Yoko Ono." Her sunglasses were just as expensive as the producer's and concealed more of her face. When Voletta asked the impresario—she called him Sean—whether she belonged on the comeback record, he reassured her that everything was under control.

✖

News leaked about a breakthrough in the search for the shooter. A *Source* magazine cover shoot was abruptly canceled when *People* committed. A prime-time interview special built anticipation for the comeback. The rapper thanked his mom, his impresario (seated at his side, of course), his fans. He referred to his bullet wounds as stigmata and called Dr. Ruben a healer. Asked whether he forgave the shooter, he hesitated before responding. He recalled Moses' conversation with the burning bush, only to interrupt himself with a stream of invective and inappropriately boisterous laughter. A coughing fit brought the interview to a premature conclusion.

Voletta declined to appear on camera.

On the strength of one of the two tracks recorded before the shooting, *Back from the Dead* sold well in its first week but it soon fizzled. The cameo appearances drowned out the main attraction. No amount of studio trickery could re-create the blow-the-house-down voice, and cognoscenti complained the star was missing from his own comeback. The rumble of yore surfaced only intermittently on what was generally regarded as a leaden affair. The impresario called a press conference and read a statement announcing the rap legend's retirement. He used the opportunity to tease the release of his new protégé's debut.

✖

Time moved on and so did all but his most devoted fans. The impresario stopped coming by.

Only Yoko Ono continued to show up. The widow of an assassinated music icon, she brought green tea that smelled like a dirty aquarium. She talked about clouds and told stories about her childhood. After the war, she said, her family had gone hungry. Neighbors starved to death; others perished from eating poison mushrooms. She would look at the clouds and make up stories in her head.

Curious, Voletta sought out her albums in Soho record stores and finally found one she put out with her husband, both of them standing naked on the cover. She decided not to pay $300 for that. A solo effort from 1973, its cover featuring Yoko's likeness superimposed on the Sphinx, set her back just $11. The songs were simple and direct, embodying feminist rage, but the vocals were harsh and incompatible with the time signatures. Her son asked her to turn it off, but she played both sides, waiting for the small voice to bubble over like lava. He tried reading one of her paperbacks but tossed it aside upon discovering the poems didn't rhyme. There's a difference between lava and a lava lamp.

Seventeen years earlier, a deranged fan had checked into a Sheraton Hotel, signing the hotel register using the name of his idol, Yoko's husband, and the next day got him to sign an album cover. That night the fan showed up at the same spot, this time wielding a .38 special, and shot him four times.

Voletta clenched her jaw, recognizing in Yoko her son's tendency to self-mythologize. His greatest hit chronicled imaginary days when there was no food on the family dinner table. When she'd confronted him, he'd told her it was just a song, but she knew people would always make assumptions about her and about all Black women.

They sat on the couch folding paper. "Tojo?" he said.

"I'm Yoko. Y-O-K-O."

"Yeah, but you feel more like a Tojo to me, okay?"

She hesitated. "Okay, Fridge."

"That's cool, Tojo. Call me Fridge. I like that." He held up an origami giraffe for her approval.

"You're going too fast. Think about each fold, make each fold perfect."

"That's deep, Tojo. Do you believe in perfection?"

"I believe in slowing down."

"That's my problem," he chuckled. "I wasn't ready to slow down. It feels like I used to be underwater, but now that I've come up for air I can't breathe. I became a fish down there, a merman, but now I'm nothing."

"It's okay to be nothing for a while."

"Yeah, Tojo. Nothing's good. Nothing means nothing wrong. Can I ask you something?"

Yoko admired the perfect crane she'd just completed.

"How much money do you have?"

"How much?"

"I mean, are you a millionaire?"

"Yes," she said, pouring them both more tea.

"How *many* millions?"

She blew on her mug and set it down. She held up ten fingers for him.

"Ten million?"

She closed her hands and then flashed them open two more times.

"You've got *thirty* million dollars?"

"That's what they tell me," she shrugged. "Not including real estate."

He called into the kitchen: "Ma, how much money do we have?"

"Sixty or seventy dollars," came the response.

"No, Ma, I mean *in the bank.* How rich are we?"

Voletta came out and stared. "How rich? We're almost a millionaire, but we owe nearly that much for this house, and we haven't even seen most of your medical bills."

"I thought the record company would take care of those.

Health insurance is supposed to be part of the whole deal."

"What record company? You're retired, remember?"

"Shit," he marveled. "Tojo's got *thirty* millions, not including real estate."

When Voletta asked her son if she should tell Yoko not to come by so often, he said it made no difference one way or the other. The tea tasted better than it smelled.

Fans scared Voletta, but her son needed their love like plants need sunlight. Whenever he went out in his wheelchair, he would sign CDs and body parts. He gave out his phone number and, sometimes, hundred-dollar bills. He would listen to their stories and come in close for hugs. She hoped that Yoko's loss would penetrate his skull.

✖

A hand-delivered letter arrived for Latitia at the *S.P.I.T.* office.

Ms. Van Eyck,

Regarding the characterization of this figure as "universally beloved," I must register at least one dissent. You probably remember Da Bronz from Da Bronx. His first two albums, GET BRONZED and DA BRONZ AGE, made the charts and the clubs. He got played on Hot 97 and appeared on YO! MTV RAPS. Because of him, black boys got their hair cut into ramp fades and white boys bought leopard-skin vests in suburban shopping malls. Da Bronz was at the top of his game in 1993. When his lips parted, flames issued from his mouth. The devil was buckled into the cockpit of his heart. He was a walking electromagnet, and the streets bent around him. The empire of hip-hop stretched out as far as the eye could see, and a voice whispered, 'Some day all this will be yours.'

And then it vanished. That tub of lard tugged
on a thread and the whole fabric unraveled,
leaving Da Bronz naked and humiliated, an
Arsenio punch line surrounded by crates of
unsold merch. Nobody called. Nobody picked up
when he called. He became nobody, all because
the Heavyweight Champion of the Borough, the
reverse alchemist, had — on a whim — turned his
name to shit.
—NAME WITHHELD

✖

"Back in my day," Yoko said. "We smoked blunts too. We
partied like rock stars."

"Yeah?"

"Of course we did. We invented that. We also marched in
the streets."

"How come?"

"To stop the War."

"How did that go?"

"The War stopped." She looked out the window. "It took
only eight years."

"How long would it have gone on if you hadn't
marched?"

"Good question. Maybe five or six."

It would be wrong, or at least an oversimplification,
to call it mentoring. The rapper was already a fully formed
artist by the time Yoko came along. He didn't need a guru,
but suffering left him temporarily open to new perspectives.
He was remaking himself. Yoko just happened to facilitate
some critical introductions. She brought him to the studio
of Marina Abramović, who asked to look at his wounds and
pronounced, "You weren't shot by a man. You were shot by
history."

"It was a n—— in a Bart Simpson mask."

The three of them bathed in a pit filled with cold coffee.

"We got to stop at Met," he said afterward. "That's where I got my start."

"The Metropolitan Museum of Art?" Yoko asked. "Or the Metropolitan Opera? They send me a letter every other day, it seems like."

"What? No. The grocery store. I used to work there as a kid."

The rock widow, head to toe in black, steered the retired rapper, resplendent in a purple robe, through the aisles of the Met Food Market. She put fresh kiwi and pears in the basket that dangled from the handles of his wheelchair.

"Do you know karate, Tojo?"

"No, do you?" Yoko laughed. "Weren't you in the Wu-Tang Clan?"

He leaned over and snagged a few boxes of Ho Hos. Two preteen boys in tracksuits approached, one with a CD for him to sign, the other empty handed, so their idol signed one of the Ho Ho boxes. Before he could continue, a tiny grandmother limped up and gave him a hug. "We never stopped loving you," she said.

"I love you too," he said, clinging to her. "This is my home. You are all my family."

Yoko pushed him to the candy aisle and helped him lower a box of Three Musketeers (not one bar, a box of 36) onto his lap. Then he remembered his mom wanted six veal chops and three cans of Campbell's Cream of Mushroom.

✖

Feeding a long strand of strawberry lace into her mouth, Latitia reread the name-withheld letter. She would have preferred to let this one go, but it already had her tangled. Every rapper had haters, but this manifestation struck her as especially virulent and specific. The backward-slanting cursive looked like it had been spun in the corner of a dark basement.

At the Tower Records around the corner from *S.P.I.T.*, she asked the clerk if he had ever heard of Da Bronz from Da Bronx. He sent her to the Lincoln Center store, where the hip-hop buyer checked several online databases and came up empty. "That doesn't automatically make him fake," he said. "There are a lot of rappers out there."

"But chart-topping?"

"True, and I doubt he ever appeared on *Yo! MTV Raps*. Maybe as an extra in a crowd scene."

Latitia was glad he didn't ask why she wanted to know. Was this for a story? Was she protecting her friend? Was he even her friend? Or did he just expect her to show up with fried shrimp from time to time?

✖

Some of Yoko's introductions fell flat. The rapper dozed off—and snored—in a Central Park West apartment when Philip Glass played E above high C a thousand times on a grand piano. He walked out of a Patti Smith New Year's Eve poetry reading and refused to let Annie Leibovitz photograph him in the nude. But he allowed himself to be seduced by sushi, Fellini, and craniosacral massage. Plus, Yoko's personal accountants devoted two full weeks to straightening out his finances and uncovered more than four million dollars.

"When I saw you yesterday," she said when she picked him up, "you were in a satin robe. Today it's Armani."

"That was a *silk* robe, Yoko."

"You're telling the Jap she doesn't know the difference between satin and silk?"

He steered his wheelchair up a ramp and into the back of what looked like an ordinary UPS truck. Yoko scampered up behind him. Inside was a black leather couch and a flat-screen television. As the rapper settled in, Yoko asked him, "Did you ever drop acid?"

"What's that?"

"LSD. It makes you hallucinate. 'Cellophane flowers of yellow and green, towering over your head.'"

"No. That's not very gangster, to be perfectly frank." He turned the TV on, and they watched one of his own music videos on mute. The younger, healthier version was getting riddled with bullets but still dancing and rapping. "Who do *you* think shot me?" he asked.

"Probably a fan, right?"

"No way, my fans *love* me." He accepted a glass of champagne proffered by an attendant staffing the wet bar.

"That's the problem. When John and I were first married, we were living on an estate in the country. Somehow, a shell-shocked G.I. found his way there and knocked on the door. He started explaining how all of John's songs were messages to him. John asked him if he was hungry and invited him in."

"Some fans are a little bit screwy."

The attendant put on one of the rapper's mixtapes, loud enough that the beats made the van bounce. After a while, Yoko signaled for him to turn it down.

"Why all the *n—— this, n—— that*?"

"It's how we talk, so it's how we rap."

"But it's not a good thing to be a n——, is it?"

"Not when *you* say it. When *we* say it, it shows respect. We're scum. We're dirt. We're all the shit white people have rejected. We recognize that in each other and remind ourselves."

"Constantly?"

"If need be."

"My husband sang, 'Woman is the n—— of the world.'"

"That's deep. If I said that I'd get lynched."

"He said he was going to get crucified."

"If I had to choose between lynching and crucifixion, I'd choose crucifixion."

"Fair enough."

"It's just a word, Toto."

"For real? No. *Green* is just a word. *Circle* and *Lilac*. But that, no, that's an assault weapon."

"I bet people called you all kinds of names when you broke up your husband's band."

"When I what? You bet. I was the yellow menace, the dragon bitch, the chink slut with the slanted snatch."

"There . . . *that*." He grinned for perhaps the first time in weeks.

"What?"

"You just *rapped*, Toto."

✖

Another letter appeared at the *S.P.I.T.* office. Like the first, it lacked a return address or postmark.

Ms. Van Eyck,

You probably deduced that I am Da Bronz. Or was. I want to provide more details about my first encounter with your friend. I was in D&D on 37th Street recording BACK TO DA BRONZ AGE, and everything was tight. The beats were hitting just right. I had written and rewritten two dozen pages full of rhymes the whole world needed. This chubby kid stumbled in. His clothes looked slept in.

"Where are your rhymes?" I asked, still not sure if he was who he said he was.

He formed his hand into a pistol and pointed his index finger at his temple. His bloodshot eyes unfocused, a slight curl on his lips.

"Cool," I said. "You memorized them."

"You could say that," he mumbled as he literally tripped on the microphone cord.

Who sent this child? I wondered as he struggled with his headphones. What is this costing me?

And then he opened his mouth.

At first, I was pleasantly surprised,
like I was seeing a toddler handle a spoon
all by himself. The kid's not bad—at least
I won't have to delete the track. Then I was
flattered, thinking to myself he must have
stayed up all night rehearsing. It was a show
of respect for the legend I had become.

He kept rapping, the rhymes tumbling out at
odd little angles like in a Cubist painting.
As he went on (and on and on), I began to go
numb, experiencing a combination of wonder
at his dexterous flow and awareness that I
was about to be shown up on my own album. And
this was before he swerved—effortlessly—into
unmistakable disses.

Rhyme assassin? / Yo, the rhyme ass is in. /
Wouldn't share a hashpipe / With this black
ass wipe / Da Bronz is a da-distant third /
He's la-la-la-lost for words / La-la-la-like a
whole bowl of unflushed turds

He looked up and caught my eye through the
studio glass. His expression was that of a
child who knows he's been naughty. A child who
deserves a spanking but firmly believes the
mischief was worth it.

I knew immediately my career was over. I
could bury this recording, but it wouldn't
stay buried. It would leak to the street
and attach a permanent stink to my name, the
account I'd built over four years of nonstop
hustle. I could feel my emptiness as Adam felt
his nakedness.

In the space of a few verses I watched
myself becoming extinct. Da Bronx went from
A-list to nameless.

✖

"I already changed music," the rapper told producer Dan the Automator, "and now I want to change it again."

Yoko's rap didn't turn up on the album they recorded, but she has some beats on it, in a way. She took him to a garage where Tom Zé was rehearsing with a troop of found-object percussionists. She joined in with a rusty sink and a pair of industrial-sized egg beaters. Then she persuaded him to slap a bicycle tire against an air conditioning duct, and they stayed past midnight.

You couldn't buy *Look Ma No Liver* in the store. You couldn't be sure you were getting the real thing. None of the participants ever confirmed its existence.

There was no lettering on the cover, just a photo of an empty red plastic basket and a sheet of paper towel dotted with crumbs and soaked through with grease. The music was hip-hop, but not hip-hop from this planet. The strain on his vocal cords imparted a new depth, new textures, to every utterance. The angst of expecting to live without his gift gave way to a morbid fascination with the squeaks and rasps that issued from his throat.

The voice was also different because his worldview had undergone emergency surgery, too. It was mature and child-like, authoritative and obscene. Instead of cracking jokes, he ran down absurd analogies. On one track, you hear him rolling seven Story Cubes before he cuts loose with *key, light, bike, fix, diamond, trophy,* and *moose,* his non sequiturs trailing off into infantile giggles. Because he had been spending so much time around his mother, her Jamaican lilt comes to the fore, along with a cornucopia of musical influences from her homeland—ska, dub, rocksteady—as well as sonic gestures from Senegal and Burundi and what sounds like Tuvan throat singing.

✖

Perched on her parked Vespa, chewing strawberry laces, Latitia lingered outside the *S.P.I.T.* offices on the off chance she might catch Da Bronz delivering another missive. Her windbreaker stuck to her skin.

Her dreadlocks had gone too long without a retwist. She had chapped lips and a ridiculous job, writing three-thousand-word essays about music that neither its creators nor audiences took seriously. It was the soundtrack to the soda commercials of a transitional generation. In a hundred years—hell, in five—nobody would care much about today's most acclaimed artists. People would mix up Vanilla Ice and Eminem. They'd remember MC Hammer and forget E-40. The magazine would fold in a year or two, and there would be no library or archive to preserve its legacy. She focused on one passerby after another, feeling nothing but disdain for their clothes, their faces, the music playing in their head-phones. She hated the sitcoms they laughed at, the plans they made and the people they made them with, the trivial thoughts bouncing around inside their skulls while they weren't listen-ing. The city was full of psychopaths, and just as she let her vigilance slip, the one she had in mind stole up behind her.

"Cowabunga, dude!" He was wearing the Bart Simpson mask again, and somehow he had looped a double strand of her strawberry lace around her throat.

"Da Bronz?"

"Let's go for a ride," he said. "Let's see if we can make it to Long Island."

"This thing might not hold us both."

"I'm more of a lightweight than you think," he assured her, pulling the lace tighter. "Not as heavy as your friend."

"Jealous much?" Latitia asked, jogging her weight to put

up the center stand and pointing her bike into the evening breeze.

" 'Jealous' misses the point," he said. "I felt jealous of emcees like Rakim, Slick Rick, and Big Daddy Kane, who schooled me in rap battles and in the studio."

"At least you have sweet taste, Da Bronz. Wish I could say the same about your breath."

"In their own way, each was a master of his craft. I'd watch them in awe and then I'd up my game. Competition among rappers can be punishing. It knocks you down and demands you stand up again for another thrashing until you learn—or cry uncle."

"You got your ass whupped one too many times."

"I could take a beating. What I couldn't deal with was the offhand, distracted manner of this slovenly pretender. Look at the way he slouches around like Jabba."

"Like who?"

"Jabba the Hutt from *Return of the Jedi.* It's like Jabba getting the Force. God should never have endowed a slob like that with the talent to rap like that."

"Great rappers," Latitia said, "stand on the shoulders of giants."

"Yeah, but they don't shit on their heads. I'm not avenging myself; I'm avenging the music, the people."

"You'll only make a martyr out of him."

"At least he'll shut his trap."

The Vespa rattling over the Williamsburg Bridge, not to mention strawberry-flavored high-fructose corn syrup constricting her carotid arteries, made conversation difficult. When they got onto the Long Island Expressway, he laughed and pulled down his mask.

"Da Bronz?"

"Yeah?"

"In your last letter, that line about watching yourself become extinct? You know that's from *Amadeus,* right?"

"From the movie, yeah. And the one about feeling my emptiness as Adam felt his nakedness is from the play. Peter Shaffer totally gets mediocrity."

They sailed past Hidden Pond's security station.

"I was just thinking," Da Bronz mused, "when I shot his buddy last year in Vegas, it was personal. I just didn't like his face."

"You kidding me? The man was beautiful like a Michelangelo statue."

"You know what I mean," he said. "The way his silent movie eyes always glistened with crocodile tears. But now that I'm preparing to take out the other one, it just sort of makes sense. The Twin Towers of hip-hop! It's time to pull them down and start again."

"Maybe you'll get a record contract."

"Nah, I'm kind of retired," he said. "I used to look up to Chuck D and KRS One; now I count Lee Harvey Oswald and James Earl Ray as my heroes, and even more whoever got away with killing Malcolm X." Without loosening his confection grip on her throat, he withdrew a 9mm pistol from the pocket of his down jacket.

"For real, Da Bronz?" Latitia was just about ready to swerve into oncoming traffic, if it meant stopping this madman.

"For real. They didn't want to destroy the revolution. They wanted to accelerate it, to move on to the next chapter. They pushed fast-forward to see what would come next."

Black smoke was coming off the Vespa as they pulled up to Voletta's house. Latitia's lip was split from the wind, and deep pink grooves ringed her neck.

✖

Inside the UPS truck, where Voletta had banished them to smoke a blunt, the rapper and the rock widow were folding paper cranes and watching footage of the Beatles at the

Hollywood Bowl.

"How did they get so big? Who was their manager?"

"A man named Brian. He told them to let their hair grow long."

"That's it? Everything's easier for white boys."

"They wore matching shirts without collars and cracked jokes at their press conferences. Brian was in love with John."

"I wish my manager had loved me a bit more. Did you see that press conference? He said it was my destiny to put out three—and only three—landmark albums."

"You know who your real beef is with?"

"Yeah, but he's dead."

"Wrong, fatso, it's your deadbeat dad."

"Eureka, Madame Butterfly, I'm cured."

"You'll see."

"Why's Tish here?" the rapper asked. "And who's that with her?" He struggled out of the couch and stepped into the yard, Yoko and a dense cloud of peace and love trailing behind him.

Da Bronz pulled up his mask, hopped off the bike, and pointed his gun. "Up against the truck," he ordered. "All of you."

"Who *is* that, Tish?" the star asked.

"I'm Bart Simpson," Da Bronz deadpanned. "Who the hell are you?"

"I'm the n—— who's gonna pop a cap in your ass."

"You have a *gun?*" Yoko fumed.

"Guess I had one or two left over." He shrugged as he and Da Bronz squared off, weapons drawn. Yoko and Latitia stood between them, the reporter stunned and mute in the widow's surprisingly strong arms.

"Put it down," Yoko commanded the rapper, pulling off her shades and training her eyes on his. "Right now."

"If I put it down, he's going to shoot me again."

"No," Yoko said. "He will not."

"Yes I will," Da Bronz asserted. "That's why I'm here."

"Take that mask off," she said without turning her head, and the would-be assassin obeyed.

"Da Bronz?" The star chuckled in disbelief.

"Yeah, man."

"How you been?"

"You know."

"I guess I do."

Latitia made a weak sound in her throat.

"What's your name?" Yoko said. "Your real name."

"Orenthal," he stammered.

"Where are you from?"

"Hartford, Connecticut, originally."

"It was all a dream, Orenthal."

"Let me shoot him, Tojo," the star said. "It's only fair."

"It was all a dream," Yoko repeated. "And now the dream is over."

"Keep talking," the rapper said. "When I say duck . . ."

"Drop your gun, Christopher," Yoko said, pointing one earpiece of her shades at his chest. "It was all a dream, remember?"

"Him first," the star said.

"Count of three," Da Bronz said.

"One," Yoko began. "Two . . ."

Just before three, a pair of white doves darted into the air, corkscrewing in the Nassau County breeze toward the setting sun, their fluttering wings glowing. In the instant that the birds—not doves, but origami cranes—distracted both gunmen, two small fists knocked loose their grips, and with a single thud two weapons dropped to the grass.

With no arms to support her, Latitia, too, collapsed on the ground.

The very next moment, Voletta stepped into the yard and announced the stew was ready.

FOR ART'S SAKE

FOR ART'S SAKE

My dear,

This letter is written to you on the water of a Malibu swimming pool, but I trust you can read it.

Your latest album arrived with a Hollywood postmark. Is that where you reside these days? At first glance, the cover was all white, and I thought it was a test pressing. On closer inspection, I could make out the words *For Art's Sake* in the lower right corner in tiny characters.

For me? You shouldn't have.

I spent a considerable part of the 1970s in blackface and what can only be called a pimp outfit—a zoot suit with matching floppy-brimmed hat and big dark shades. My Black male alias: Art Nouveau. Often seen in the company of Don Alias (his real last name), an actual Black man who drummed for Nina Simone, Miles Davis, Lou Reed, Roberta Flack, and Marianne Faithfull, among others.

Don wasn't with me that night by the pool. A song was born that night that was not sung for another fifteen years.

✖

The record begins with the electric sizzle of a microphone being switched on, followed by a prolonged hacking cough, as though you're clambering out of a pool, chlorine searing your throat. "Wait a minute, wait a minute," you mutter. I hear you spit out something viscous and sniff moistly before reciting a declaration taken from Heloise's first letter to Abelard, dating from the twelfth century: "If Augustus, Emperor of the whole world, thought fit to honor me with marriage and conferred all the earth on me to possess forever, it would be dearer and more honorable to me to be called not his Empress but your whore." The final word comes out in a leering drawl.

A tom-tom-driven four-on-the-floor beat stumbles forth, joined by three or four horns in delirious syncopation. A falsetto cry breaks in, twisting and bobbing in a jet stream of sustained notes played on an electric organ. The brass and percussion drop out, and the vocal soars higher and resolves into a fluttering elastic yawp.

I use the lever to lift the tone arm, letting the record continue to spin a centimeter below the dusty stylus.

✱

Something is happening to my skin that isn't quite decomposition. Maybe these words are alive, or will become animated, momentarily, if and when somebody reads them, like a fly struggling on flypaper.

First I itched like mad, and then it became truly maddening. My condition hasn't been studied. The medical establishment dismisses it as imaginary. Yet fibers in a variety of colors protrude out of my skin, like mushrooms after a rainstorm. They cannot be forensically identified as animal, vegetable, or mineral.

Chain-smoking by day, chain-wanking by night, I have spent three February weeks in this fireplace-heated Saskatoon mansion. During this time I have eaten nothing but a Three

Musketeers bar and a tin of lobster bisque. The house contains neither a guitar nor a pen, but it has a typewriter and a sheaf of paper that I am using to continue our correspondence. I haven't dreamed. I haven't changed out of my long johns, blue jeans, and undyed cable-knit wool sweater.

And the record spins on.

✱

We aren't Heloise and Abelard; we're Pyramus and Thisbe, lovers divided by a wall. On one side, a Black man in the process of metamorphosing into a white woman. On the other, a white woman posing as a Black man. Here, a grief-punctured heart still beating. There, a healthy one craving death.

The wall is something we share. The wall is love. The hole in the wall, if we can both find it, is the ultimate love song.

✱

Ever since 1957, when Bo Diddley recorded you and your band the Marquees in D.C., you loved the studio. It was a playhouse, a club, a special sort of laboratory, and a place of retreat from your father, a Pentecostal minister who beat you mercilessly and also liked to parade around in women's clothes, the more outlandish the better.

Your greatest hit became a raisin commercial, but since you didn't write the music or lyrics but only made the song world famous, you didn't receive a dime of the ad income.

What's Going On (1971) is deservedly acknowledged as your best album. Like another all-time great, *Thriller*, it contains only nine songs. Ironically, both albums are at least one track too long. Your masterpiece doesn't need "Save the Children," while *Thriller* could do without "The Lady in My Life"—which is not to detract from either one.

Your best composition? "Trouble Man," from the 1972 album of the same name. (Actually, the album had a subtitle,

"Don't Mess with Mister 'T'," long before Mr. T the bouncer-turned-actor came along.) "Trouble Man" has had a curious second life courtesy of female singers, including Neneh Cherry, Rickie Lee Jones (who some call my doppelgänger, but I don't see it), Angie Stone, and myself (on the debut album of Kyle Eastwood, son of Clint). It sounds like we women are phrasing the first line as *"I've come apart"* (suggestive of a psychic break) rather than *"I come up hard"* (testimony to growing up in poverty). Misheard lyrics, mondegreens, can be humorous—like "S'cuse me while I kiss this guy"—but here it's an artistic choice.

I come apart. That's what's happening to me. Unraveling.

✖

"Marrying a queen might not make me a king," you once said about Anna Gordy, sister of Motown founder Berry Gordy. "But at least I'd have a shot at being a prince."

A prince.

When you married, you were 24 and she was 41. The raisin commercial song originally went out to Anna, who had repeatedly strayed. The marriage lasted until 1973, when you took your next bride, 16-year-old Janis Hunter. Your second wife was 34 years younger than your first.

As part of the divorce with Anna, you agreed to give her a portion of the royalties from your next album. *Here, My Dear* flopped, and at the time people believed you had deliberately made it bad so she would get less money. But over time it became a fan and critical favorite, due to its painful candor.

"If you don't honor what you said," you admonish her, "you lie to God."

You inherited cross-dressing from your father. "Seeing myself as a woman is something that intrigues me," you confessed to your biographer. "It's also something I fear. I indulge myself only at the most discreet and intimate moments.

Afterward, I must bear the guilt and shame for weeks."
Without shame there can be no pleasure.

Duets were your forte. You had a series of them—and
allegedly a passionate affair—with Tammi Terrell. You sang
"Ain't No Mountain High Enough," "Ain't Nothing Like
the Real Thing," and "You Ain't Livin' Till You're Lovin'"
together and then in 1967, Terrell fainted onstage, and you
caught her in your arms. After she died from a brain tumor
in 1970, your almost gave up music, suddenly becoming convinced you would make a great wide receiver for the Detroit
Lions, despite never having played on a football team, not
even in high school.

You and I never duetted, technically, but in a more important way we did. Just as kissing is more intimate than
fucking, singing with someone is more intimate than dancing with them. One mouth is a mere organ, but two together
make an orgasm, a miracle. You don't sing (or kiss) with just
your lips or tongue. Teeth, cheeks, and jaw all play a part,
even nose and throat. What else could you call this decade-
long yet unconsummated romance, this deadly duel, but a
demonic duet?

✖

I was no virgin. On the contrary, I'd had ample experience
loving and being loved. I had broken big hearts into little
pieces. I had gone over and over the edge of mad romance,
courting risk and sparking betrayal for the sake of a song.
Love was my food and my god, my addiction and my
Olympics. I could trace every rhyme in my discography to a
specific kiss or bruise. *Don Juan's Reckless Daughter* would
have been a fitting title for any of my albums.

Nobody in history knew a love song like I did, but *Here,
My Dear* struck me like a slow-motion thunderbolt. Every
note plucked a string in my guts. Every beat resounded in my

chest cavity. The lyrics were etched upon my sex long before the needle settled into the groove.

A few rare albums had stunned me into silence before. *Blonde on Blonde* freezer-burnt my nether regions and *Astral Weeks* coated my throat and lungs with black mold. *Hot Buttered Soul* sent me into anaphylactic shock. Still, I gave as good as I got, reducing great songwriters—Zimmerman, Cohen, Simon—to tantrums. (And not just Jews; I saw James Taylor's tears, and Neil Young's, up close.) This was different. *Here, My Dear* stripped my words and my music apart, exposing the folly of unknown tunings, the fatuousness of my naïf poetics, the fraud of the whole bohemian persona.

✷

At the dawn of the 1980s, we saw each across an empty swimming pool at a Malibu party thrown by a mutual mogul friend. Moonlight, pool lights, and the siren song of cocaine enclosed us in a magical aura as our eyes met. We were both so beautiful it might have been heaven.

We never spoke, not at the party, and not afterwards—not even the time I saved your life—but I have it on good authority that you made inquiries. You bought all my albums, didn't you? My lyrics might have sailed right by you, but my voice grabbed you by the balls and sent yours up an octave. Musically, I met your Casanova gaze with a Medusa reflection.

You yearned to pair my voice with yours, to forge new harmonies and climb the charts with an unprecedented Black-white, male-female duet.

"There was somebody at the party I'd never seen before," you told your manager.

"You want me to get her number?"

"Not her. Him. I've never seen anybody like this. I need this person in my life."

"You said a male-female duet."

"Right, but I didn't say which one *I* was. This isn't going to be like my other duets. It's a true collaboration, where each of us surrenders control to the other. We trade ideas, we trade identities, we become each other."

"Cool."

"Don't patronize me. This goes beyond music. It's metaphysics."

When your calls and letters went unanswered (sorry, I was never good about getting back to people), you trusted happenstance to bring us together. You never gave up. I became a kind of goddess to you. You listened obsessively in secret, alone in a studio you had expressly built for this purpose.

You made extensive preparations for my arrival, learning to play fretless bass like Jaco Pastorius and soprano saxophone like Wayne Shorter. You would be the only instrument I needed. Play *me*, you prayed. You rebuilt and redecorated the studio, emblazoning the walls with Georgia O'Keeffe motifs and importing original Bauhaus furniture.

We're all sensitive people, you sang. But maybe some of us are just a tad more sensitive than the rest.

In your obsessive preparations, if you couldn't decide what I'd want, you put on my clothes and makeup and asked the mirror. (But honey child, painted toes and patterned hose just won't do.) It wasn't just opening yourself up to my influence. The more you studied me, the more you noticed of yourself. "Not me, but it's not bad," you'd smile. Distractedly listening to the radio one afternoon, you caught a bit of one of your own hits and supposed it was my voice on the airwaves.

✖

We followed each other around town like a couple of private dicks assigned to one another by a prankster. I spotted you coming out of Trader Vic's with Berry Gordy, but I was with a very high David Crosby and didn't trust him to behave.

You started to approach me at the 1981 Grammys, but you veered away at the last second. In 1982, we came close to singing our duet. My band and I had just finished the one with the line (so to speak) "Couldn't you just love me like you love cocaine" when my manager, the mogul, called from the back of his limousine, using one of the very first mobile phones. "It's on for tomorrow," he declared.

"He said yes?"

"We never heard back. This guy is better."

"I don't like the sound of that. Nobody's better."

"Bigger. More of a hit maker."

"Let's just try him one more time."

"You didn't even ask who we found. You don't want the other one. He doesn't make hits anymore. He makes trouble."

"That's what I want."

"Have you seen Zeffirelli's *Endless Love*? Brooke Shields in the altogether?"

"Why are you talking about child pornography? Were you talking on another line?"

"We got Lionel Richie. You don't know how hard that was."

"I explicitly asked for the Trouble Man, and you got me that horse-face cheesemonger? I asked for Carrera marble, and you're giving me that block of feta?"

The next day, Lionel and my band—including my new bassist husband—waited in the studio. The hours ticked by, each of them costing the label a small fortune. They ordered Chinese. They played poker. They fiddled with the settings, switching amplifiers and pickups.

Finally, I showed up, three hours late. Or Art Nouveau did. Or maybe it was the soul man I'd invited, joining horse face for my song about flat tires.

✱

Songs are codes, heard by millions, understood by one. Each new song, while ostensibly addressed to the love object, responds to past songs with similar chord changes, rhyme schemes, and lyrical conceits echoing back to the *ur*-song, which may have been simian or even avian.

The Monkees. The Byrds.

Hits are codes traded back and forth on radio waves and pop charts, smuggled into magazine interviews and passed along surreptitiously via unsuspecting interlocutors. We both developed a hypersensitivity to these messages, interpreting chance gestures and unrelated utterances and concocting ever more convoluted responses. If someone asked us to describe our correspondence, no doubt our summaries would diverge more than they converged, but both would be perfectly accurate. These fibers coming out of my skin are painful codes from you, emerging from inside of my body. The colors are quite wonderful, though. I shall have them woven into a garment that I wear, as a code just for you.

Cocaine is a song. It stood at the top of the charts from 1977 (the year Studio 54 opened and Eric Clapton released his valentine to the drug) until 1982, the year it killed John Belushi.

Cocaine is a code, danceable and catchy. What does it mean? It's God's way of telling you you're making too much money, as Robin Williams joked. Fair enough, but who cares what He's saying? God is talking to you.

✳

Sr. continued to torment you as your career took off; he scorned your musical gifts. He followed you from show to show, berating you backstage for your unmanly falsetto. He barged into the studio, attempting to steal or destroy the master recordings. He took special pleasure in leaking gossip and lies to eager reporters. And then one day it went too far. Or almost did. I happened to be in the neighborhood (okay, I was stalking) when Sr. entered your home, demanding money and waving the .38 caliber Smith & Wesson you had given him as a present.

Suicidally depressed and deep into a cocaine binge, you insulted Sr.'s aim and dared him to prove you wrong.

"Don't test me, son."

"Don't tease me, Dad. *If you don't honor what you said, you lie to—*"

Sr. raised his gun and had started to squeeze the trigger when Art Nouveau burst in. Distracted, Sr. shot wide of the mark, shattering a Tiffany lamp.

"Who the hell are you?" Sr. bellowed.

"I'm Art, man," Art said. "Put the weapon down."

Sr. aimed the gun at Art, then at you, and then, calmly, took it into his mouth and blew his own brains out.

✖

Traumatized, you dropped from view after that, but I always knew you'd make your comeback. Alone in my Saskatoon retreat, I finally lower the stylus back onto the spinning platter.

The coughing fit is a feint for fans worried about your health. In fact your delivery is as powerful and precise as ever, as you prove over eleven brief, delicate, thematically and texturally interrelated songs. It is an impressionistic song cycle closer, frankly, to my oeuvre than to any R&B or soul precedent, gauzy reminiscences shot through with regret. A haunting melodic figure plucked on a jazz guitar resurfaces later on an accordion. Street names and bible verses recur, alternating with dialogue appropriated from noir films.

The sound is so vivid I can see it in Technicolor.

The soul singer has begun to resemble a raisin, shrunken and desiccated. This irony does not occur to you as you slide back the bolt on the door of your secret home studio.

A frail silhouette in a long pearlescent gown, lit only by a red RECORDING IN PROGRESS sign, you lean against the console, catching your breath after the effort of unbolting. You remain perfectly still, eyes closed, trying to tune into the broadcast of a recalcitrant muse.

Surrounding you are pictures of yours truly, clipped from fashion and music magazines. My face. My body. My quotations transcribed in a shaky hand, dog-eared covers of my albums. Imitations of scarves I've worn and other approximations of my carefully casual style hang from clothespins. Nobody but you has ever entered this shrine, but I can see it in my mind's eye.

Plopping down on a piano bench, you tap out a few jazzy chords before letting your unsteady fingers slide off the keys. An unplugged Fender bass yields a similarly meager harvest. You fumble with the microphone switch and inadvertently record a coughing fit that dissolves into heaving sobs that topple a stack of tape spools.

On the floor with the tapes, you appear to slump into a doze, your gaunt frame softly rising and falling, but after ten motionless minutes you spring up with surprising energy, walk over to an upended drum kit, and pull the hem of the gown up over your bony knees. The eraser ends of two Ticonderoga pencils thump rapid patterns on the snare, coaxing your hips and backbone into a writhing trance that makes the silk shimmer. Owling to verify that the RECORDING light remains on, you emit a wavering falsetto hum—a pencil sketch, if you will, for your first posthumous song.

Remorse courses through your comeback album. You know you are a sinner and refuse to make excuses for your tangled yet consistent history of betrayal, deceit, and self-ishness. You have been cruel, careless, and hypocritical, and you no longer believe music can expiate sin. Confession, apology, and reconciliation are private activities, and any attempt at setting them to melody drains their value. All you can do is resume your musical career as someone else, unswerving in the glare of your new self-knowledge. You make the album in order to discover what your newly humbled self sounds like.

Although later musicologists will attempt to credit an array of backing instrumentalists, in fact you build each song in utter solitude, patiently layering track upon self-recorded track. *For Art's Sake* is the sound of a bearded genius queen alone in the dark.

"Who was that lady I saw you with last night?"

"That was no lady, that was myself."

✱

Late in 1986, *For Art's Sake* shipped to record stores across the country. Unapologetically vulgar, gleefully mixing metaphors and inventing portmanteaux with reckless abandon, you seem to be making the lyrics up as you go along, but you stick every rhyme. The music keeps pace throughout, effortlessly evoking a Dixieland whorehouse one moment and a Hollywood soirée the next.

At the end of the second side, a pistol explodes, unleashing a five-minute flood of futuristic funk, sirens (the sound created by Stevie Wonder's harmonica, it will be claimed), and echo-drenched whimpers of pain.

Largely because of its lyrical transgressions, *For Art's Sake* got very little radio play. This was, after all, the height of the Parents Music Resource Center's crusade against obscenity. It was also blessedly out of step with 1980s pop, featuring natural drums and dry analogue engineering. An obviously jealous Prince told *Rolling Stone,* "Marvin's dad shoulda aimed better."

Prince, the sole artist who could rightly be called our love child. That's what really hurt, but *For Art's Sake* so obviously mapped the course of the rest of his career that I could hardly hold a grudge. Now he's gone, too, the teenager with the huge eyes who sat in the front row of my concerts and wrote me so many unanswered letters.

The cover isn't blank white. It's a close-up of a brick of cocaine. Or is it a block of marble?

✖

Thousands of miles away, I lie supine on your studio floor, kissing the mouth that sang the raisin commercial. It's like caressing Michelangelo's marble. It's like being caressed by the chisel.

And I'm just about to lose my mind.

Yours,
Joni

DISGRACED

For Hal Willner

DISGRACED

Upon learning of the death of his father, whom he'd met just once, he reclaimed the name on his birth certificate. Scott had been an unhappy, confused child, but as Jeff, life became not only tolerable but downright ecstatic. His undeniable talent lit up the world in new, crazed colors. When he sang, the birds stopped what they were doing and paid heed.

When not creating music, he listened to it every waking moment. Nusrat Fateh Ali Khan, Nina Simone, Marvin Gaye, Edith Piaf, Robert Plant. Family, friends, and lovers gave him endless leeway. His beautiful appearance didn't hurt, either. The road ahead had been cleared of distraction and complication.

His debut record arrived fully formed in the world, a swashbuckling and utterly cinematic classic. Everybody who heard it fainted at least twice. Many of them awoke with its lyrics tattooed across their torsos.

Jeff felt no pressure about his sophomore album. He loved his sidemen, but they were replaceable. Producers mattered only for singers not blessed with a larynx like his. As far as he was concerned, the gods had created him for the following day, when he would walk into the studio and let the Day-Glo curlicue patterns issue from his throat. Soon, through the magic of recording technology and the music industry supply chain, it would boom out of speakers all over the world.

To his friends, the buildup to the session had looked erratic. He had tried and failed to buy a house that wasn't for sale. He had applied for a job as butterfly keeper at the Memphis Zoo. Yet each seemingly irrational act made perfect sense in the context of the songs gestating inside him. The world would understand before long.

A sudden urge sent him fully clothed into Wolf River Harbor. Faux zebra-skin wingtip boots hugged his calves, their square toes jutting out of the murky water. Floating on his back, he serenaded a roadie with a Zeppelin song about the glorious end of the world. Crows wheeled overhead, and sheet lightning blinked to a disco beat.

And then a whirlpool jerked him straight down to the bottom. The lining of his lungs and throat burned with muddy water. The heat scarring his insides came from deep within the earth. He welcomed this internal, eternal, infernal force down his gullet. He greeted it with worship and praise. Hallelujah.

Certain of death, he swallowed gulp after gulp of liquid fire. Wading into the Mississippi hadn't been a suicidal act, but now that he was *in* the river, his resolve hardened.

No wonder there were so many gospel songs about rivers. The water moved you; it moved with you and through you. You could sit on the bank and watch the flow, or you could *be* the flow. And the flow was eternity.

But something went wrong at that moment of crystalline darkness, and he did not die.

A muscled, reddish (if color vision can be trusted under dirty rushing water) arm, heavily tattooed, flashed like a bolt of underwater lightning, and a grip crushed his dainty wrist. A humanoid face, twisted in a contemptuous grimace, appeared through the haze of bubbles, eyes glittering black against Coca-Cola-colored cloud formations.

The air that had been trapped in Jeff's lungs erupted out his mouth and nose with a sound that was half-sneeze, half-roar. Malicious laughter filled the air, leaving a dull hiss hanging as he found himself alone on the riverbank.

He remained there, sunk on all fours in Mississippi mud, too spent to shiver, saturated with regrettable survival and yet grateful for the dark beast that had saved him.

✖

He felt more than heard the calling. He would sing for Satan from this moment on. The voice that had animated his spirit for as long as he could remember—it now belonged to the fallen angel Lucifer. Of course it did. There had never been anything celestial about it.

Basking in the knowledge that Hell was real and that Satan had sired his soul, he rose and struggled toward a dimly throbbing orange light on the horizon.

He roamed an unfamiliar hamlet, hearing sounds he had never noticed before. A beer truck struggling down a long driveway. An air conditioning unit shuddering on. Three men arguing about Vietnam. It was the first time in a long time he'd been somewhere without music playing.

Denim scratching canvas. The soles of his waterlogged boots glancing against the pavement, the air sucking in and out of his lungs. The multidirectional rhythm could not be contained by his mind, making it hard for him to continue walking but impossible for him to stop.

But then there *was* music. It was harsh and repetitive, but it was music, live music, not recorded, and he followed the sound through a junk-littered brownfield to a ramshackle warehouse with pentagrams spray-painted on the side. The volume hit him with gale force. Just like the river, it penetrated his body.

"Who's there?" came an irritated grumble as the music ground to a halt. He stood in the doorway, and once his eyes adjusted he could make out three figures—two with guitars and one behind a drum kit.

Negoniack (sometimes spelled Niggoniact or N'gon Yak) was already legendary in poor white areas of Tennessee, Arkansas, northern Mississippi, and southern Missouri. Their infamous pitch-dark concerts are remembered to this day, although seldom talked about. No lighters or phones were permitted. Electrical tape covered all the equipment displays and even, when the authorities weren't checking, the exit signs. Every Sunday night, a thousand-plus head-bangers and thrill seekers paid five dollars apiece to experience Negoniack in spaces meant to hold two hundred fifty. Their performances—it would be more accurate to call them rituals—lasted hours, and nobody was allowed to enter once they'd begun or leave before they ended. Assuming the name Brimstone, Jeff took on vocal duties.

The bass guitarist, a lanky virtuoso with Pre-Raphaelite hair and a peach-fuzz mustache, let Brimstone stay on his couch. Every morning he split a dozen eggs and a dozen beers with his guest. The band members socialized exclusively with one another, but there wasn't much conversation. In between marathon rehearsals, they watched Japanese cartoons and professional wrestling. Their only other hobby was covering each other's skin with tarot-inspired tattoos.

Besides vocals, Jeff brought Grand Guignol flair to the proceedings. As black lights bathed the stage, he produced a live white rat, occasionally a kitten or dove, from a wicker basket and tossed it to the throng to be torn apart. (Just before surrendering the animal, he'd drop it back into the basket and substitute a cheap prop, a surgical glove coated with cotton candy and filled with raspberry jam.)

Recordings circulated on unmarked black cassettes. Most lacked even pauses to distinguish one blast of noise from the next. Their audio quality ranged from staticky to sludgy, but one tape—known alternately as *Unholy Sacrifice* and *Sacrificial Host*—gradually acquired a following beyond the satanic metal community.

Meanwhile, Jeff's mother fought the record company's plans to release the demos he had recorded for his second album. No body had been washed up, and she was hoping for a miracle.

✖

Around this time, in the western suburbs of Illinois, a mechanical engineer named Todd moved into a studio apartment not far from where his parents lived with his younger brother Rusty, whose neurological disease prevented him from responding to virtually any nonmusical communication. Todd and Rusty shared a passion for metal and other extreme musical forms. Black Sabbath and Motörhead were merely appetizers for import-only albums by Nordic and South American ensembles.

Todd burned his brother a CD almost every week. A favorable response—head bobbing, fingers wiggling—elated him, while indifference left him feeling he had failed in his most crucial responsibility. He brought his engineering skills to bear on the transitions between tracks, and over time he learned to manipulate the tracks themselves, shifting the pitch or punching up the percussion to stimulate his brother's aural nerves.

Rusty loved Ministry, but Revolting Cocks left him cold. He delighted in Foetus but rejected Nine Inch Nails.

When a coworker turned Todd on to Negoniack, he knew his brother would go crazy for them, but the pervasive hiss on the black cassette he'd borrowed compelled him to dissect and reassemble the recording before including it on a compilation for Rusty. He spent hours digitizing and scrubbing the sound of each separate instrument and unburying the sulphuric vocals, which reminded him of something he had once heard in an altogether different context.

Waves of feedback nearly submerge Brimstone's keening, "She swims to the side, the sun sees her dried" and "Freezing red deserts turn to dark, energy here in every part," both couplets lifted from songs on the Rolling Stones' *Their Satanic Majesties Request.* (Besides the obvious allure of the title, it is the album that bears the heaviest stamp of Brian Jones, rock's most famous drowning victim.) Brimstone delivers the lyrics in an altogether different melody and cadence from the original.

Rusty was growing impatient for a new CD, or at least Todd imagined he was, but this project stretched out into ten days of painstaking labor, until finally he transferred the file to a disc and brought it to the house. Their parents' Volvo wasn't in the driveway. The garbage can was capsized, its contents spread all over the lawn. Todd found his brother unbathed and cowering under an oily tarp in the garage.

In the ensuing days, with repeated visits from the police and social services, Todd never got the chance to play the re-engineered Negoniack recording for Rusty. When he came across the unplayed CD-R several months later, he snapped it in half—gashing his left thumb so badly that he had to get five stitches—and deleted the file from his computer.

✱

Years later, an unassuming-looking middle-aged man in white overalls and zebra-patterned boots drags a hand cart to his usual spot on the boardwalk on Mackinac Island in Michigan. His cart contains a queen-sized Garfield comforter, a reconditioned karaoke machine, a black top hat for collecting change, and a wicker basket with three white rats named Aoede, Melete, and Mneme. His hair now thin, shoulders rounded, hands atremble, the man no longer goes by Brimstone or even Jeff. He is Scott again, and he seldom speaks, except to young children and old ladies passing by.

As he sets up his equipment, the rats scamper about on the comforter, but once the music starts, they form an equilateral triangle and await his signal. Scott's diction is slurred, but the tones are pure that issue from his throat.

SNOW, MILK, AND PSALMS

SNOW, MILK, AND PSALMS

ABSTRACT

The death of Lhasa de Sela on January 1, 2010, coincided with a number of bizarre phenomena worldwide. This paper recounts ten such occurrences in a dispassionate, academically professional manner, with an open mind but without undue speculation. Hopeful that this catalogue will occasion further inquiry into unexplored—and unexplained—aspects of the singer's extramusical legacy, the author leaves the question of causality to future researchers.

Lhasa de Sela was born in Big Indian, New York, on September 27, 1972, and died in Montreal, Canada, on January 1, 2010. She recorded just three albums, winning a large and devoted following, mostly in Europe. Neither her biography nor her music will be addressed in this paper, though the author readily admits he is a frequent and enthusiastic listener. Although far less famous than artists like Elvis Presley, Jimi Hendrix, Frank Sinatra, or Billie Holiday, Lhasa (the author has taken the liberty of using this familiar mononym here rather than the customary *de Sela*) possessed a comparable essence that can only be described as soulful or, let's just say it, spiritual. It is this perhaps ineffable quality that has led fans as well as students of the paranormal to investigate a range of unexplained phenomena and to post their findings on various ephemeral message boards.

I should note that while it is standard practice in academic publications to credit the research of others, to follow such a convention in this case would pose a number of difficulties, including the definitive establishment of authorship and the potential for exposing the identity of the posters against their wishes. Where relevant, the author will indicate his own role in these inquiries; if no such mention is made, he entreats the reader not to assume he is claiming any credit. On the contrary, he is most grateful to this community — an overused word when it comes to message boards, but one that happens to fit here.

Here, then, are ten unexplained phenomena that coincide or correlate with the death of Lhasa de Sela:

- *Snow* — Although January snowfall is hardly uncommon in Montreal, a four-day blizzard is exceptional. Many of Lhasa's friends and musical associates noted the quality as well as the quantity of the snow that covered the city in the first four days of 2010, one saying it had a particular warmth: "When people say 'a blanket of snow,' they don't generally mean that it feels like lovingly knit wool on your cheek, but this snow did."

- *Milk* — In the late winter and early spring after Lhasa's death (or disappearance, as some prefer to call it), milk from the dairy farms of Quebec was said to have acquired a strange, subtle undertaste. The same volume was produced, with the same nutritional composition, but it generated a slight tingle on the tongue. Some detected a hint of ashtray, while others said mushrooms or feet.

Not everybody noticed, but many children did, perhaps because of their more sensitive taste receptors, perhaps because they drink more milk than adults. Although many complained or even tried returning the product to the grocery store, once the taste went away, some milk drinkers claimed to miss it.

- *Deterioration*—An art conservator on one listserv makes a compelling case involving the onset of accelerated decay in the paintings of Danish artist Vilhelm Hammershøi (1864-1916). His artworks, described by comedian and television presenter Michael Palin as "a weird but heady fusion of Vermeer and Edward Hopper," are considered to be relatively stable compared to others of a similar age. Hammershøi was nothing if not methodical, using, it is said, more than forty different kinds of white in a single canvas. Since 2010, however, many of his paintings have evinced a craquelure that was not previously apparent. Similar degradation has been detected in the photographs of Francesca Woodman and on surviving prints of Mexican wrestler films from the 1950s and 1960s.

- *Psalm*—Upon Lhasa's death, an additional psalm came into being. Did Lhasa write it? No, her death revealed it. Radiocarbon and other paleographic methods fail to register certain passages materializing post-publication, but mystics and other technicians of the sacred (to use Jerome Rothenberg's phrase) have detected such insertions again and again, especially in non-Western and pre-Gutenberg sources. Every atom in the universe is in constant motion; why should ancient documents be any different? Think of it as the million-monkeys-with-a-million-typewriters experiment, but on a non- or indeed anti-Cartesian plane: the new verse was etched, or inked, or printed in every Bible, in every alphabet—even, retroactively, in the libidinous, treacherous hand of King David himself. Exegesis and commentary instantaneously populated every reference. Different hypotheses point to different psalms as the new-comer, the majority citing what is now known as number 32 ("Blessed is he whose transgression is forgiven, whose sin is covered"), but an increasingly adamant contingent insisting on number 69 ("Save me, O God; for the waters are come in unto my soul"). The author anchored his mas-ter's of divinity thesis on the latter argument; as of this writing, the degree has not yet been granted.

- *Unease*—According to an admittedly contested reading of a massive data trove leaked in January 2013, a rift was felt in the emotional space between young lovers at the time of Lhasa's death. There is no other logical explanation, many contend, for the enhanced duration and intensity of the unease that arose the first time one said something face-tious and the other couldn't tell if it was a joke or not.

- *Cash*—On January 2, 2010, every pregnant sixteen-year-old in the Americas found three crisp $100 bills in the small front pocket of her jeans. (How could that not be Lhasa?) In most cases, the largesse was welcome, with many beneficiaries finding themselves able to buy cribs and other supplies. Unfortunately, this phenomenon has been linked to at least two murders, both in Guatemala.

- *Doom*—Some commentators read significance into the fact that Lhasa died young on New Year's Day like both Hank Williams (1923-1953) and Townes Van Zandt (1944-1997). It has been said that this trio has now "spiritually merged" (not my words) into a "tragic song formation" (ditto) that has lain heavy around the Earth ever since. Devotees of this theory have ascribed 2010's various di-sasters to Lhasa's death, including the Eyjafjallajökull volcano eruption, the Haitian earthquake, and the BP oil spill in the Gulf of Mexico. While not disputing the existence of a doom-like entity, the author feels obliged to note that Maurice Chevalier and Patti Page—two of the cheeriest singers ever—also died on New Year's Day.

- *Heritage*—In the spring thaw of 2010, the earth yielded up at least three intact and flawless Sèvres porcelain goblets. Amateur archaeologists uncovered these anomalous, exceedingly rare 18th-century objects in Idaho, Ottawa, and Latvia and brought them to local museums for analysis. Who knows how many other goblets were found at this time and simply kept?

- *Regeneration*—The cave splayfoot salamander, thought to be extinct since 1941, reappeared in 2010, as did the Mount Nimba reed frog and the Omaniundu reed frog, the last of which had previously been seen in 1967 and 1979, respectively. Lhasa's death seems to have activated dormant genetic material in remote, unlit regions.

- *Jimmy Scott*—Making a slight alteration to the history of popular music may be a relatively minor matter compared with enhancing a canonical Old Testament text, which entailed updating not just Bibles but commentaries, curricula, and the memories of scholars. Yet the insertion of Jimmy Scott into the jazz canon was no mean feat. The recordings themselves and the development of a fabulous backstory both demanded considerable skill. Scott was born in Cleveland in 1925 with a rare condition that prevented the onset of puberty; his voice never changed. Nonetheless he married five times. "Early on," he told his biographer, "I saw my suffering as my salvation." Scott pursued a vocal career and won acclaim from, among others, Billie Holiday, Marvin Gaye, and Ray Charles, who said he had "more pain and prettiness in his voice than any singer anywhere." Music industry travails nipped his career in the bud, however, and he returned to Ohio and found work as an elevator operator.

Here is where Scott's story shades into fairytale, a genre that, as fans know, captivated Lhasa from a young age. In 1991, nearly thirty years after the vocalist's retirement, filmmaker David Lynch gave him a prominent scene in *Twin Peaks*, the TV series that flopped at first but became a cult favorite. Thrust into the spotlight, the tiny old man continued to sing his heart out, releasing a string of haunting interpretations of standards as well as contemporary pop gems such as Prince's "Nothing Compares 2 U." (Madonna once said, "Jimmy Scott is the only singer who makes me cry.") When Lhasa's career launched in 1997, nobody seemed to notice her voice's resemblance to Scott's, the furious beatitude of a burning martyr present in every vowel. Of course not, and the reason wasn't that they represented different genders and genres. It was simply that Scott did not yet exist; he would not come into being until January 1, 2010. In this light, one might fairly maintain that his oeuvre—which dates back to the late 1940s and extends up to his final recording, made in 2014—should be considered appendicular to Lhasa's.

If further research can substantiate even half of the phenomena attributed to Lhasa's death, the countless hours this author has poured into this project will not be in vain.

THE SQUARE 65 MIXTAPE

"Don't call it a comeback—I been here for years."
—LL Cool J

"I'm always making a comeback, but nobody ever tells me where I've been."
—Billie Holiday

THE SQUARE 65 MIXTAPE

Cunningly the trumpeter played them all, one by one and nation against nation, intuiting then exploiting their vanities and vulnerabilities.

"Didn't I tell you, when we made *Blue Train* together, that I would always stick with you?" he asked.

"No," Coltrane replied, "but we've both been through a lot since then."

"Addiction ate a hole in my soul. Won't you forgive my past iniquities and nurse the spark within me? I will abase myself. I will comply with any demand. The more humiliating the better."

"That won't be necessary." All trumpeters were divas, desperate for approval and yet convinced of their godliness. Coltrane had learned to take it in stride.

"Your wisdom may exceed that of Bird himself. And I'm not the only one who thinks so."

Helmed by King Charlie Parker and Queen Billie Holiday, Jazz Island boasted a highly sophisticated citizenry and a bounteous treasury. Its inhabitants prized lyric poetry and haute cuisine, nuanced scholarship and athletic prowess.

Coltrane presided over a university that embodied the most refined academic and egalitarian principles.

"There must be a way to prove your superiority once and for all."

"What did you have in mind?"

"Me? Nothing. Sidemen don't have ideas."

"No?"

"Well, as a matter of fact, I may have come up with a little something. Maybe you'd be interested in hearing it."

The trumpeter undid the clasps of his case, but the master had disappeared down the corridor before he got the mouthpiece to his lips.

✖

The Flipside is a cramped used record store beneath Times Square. Everything you'd ever want to hear is here, and then some. Albums are arranged alphabetically and divided by genre. Over the years, the territory occupied by any given genre expands or contracts. Rock splits into classic and punk. Hip-hop arises and quickly occupies a sizable expanse. Easy listening fades. Country shrinks and grows and shrinks again.

These fluctuations are the product of tastes and trends, as well as ineffable qualities like genius, romance, and myth. The dead, especially the young dead, loom large here.

Whom the gods love dies young, wrote Menander in ancient times, and hoo doggie, did the gods love them some jazz or what? And they sure must have had some special affection for hip-hop, too. Across the bay from Jazz Island stood the city-state of Hiphopabad, with the impregnable Thugz Mansion at its center.

Both nations exist in the Flipside, which maps exactly onto the record store that bears its name. The continental drift of genres across crates mirrors territorial skirmishes and international intrigue in their world.

This is the unauthorized account of how Jam Master Jay claimed the Flipside crown and the part played by Lee Morgan in his ascension.

✖

Distractedly, the trumpeter let the mug of jasmine tea grow cold on his desk. Wearing a brocade robe and matching slippers, he sat alone between two emerald lampshades in an oak-paneled conservatory. Stone-faced though hardly serene, he held the pencil point suspended a few inches above a clean sheet of staff paper. He wasn't waiting for the muse. That crucial visitation had taken place while he was still alive, and the composition already existed fully formed in his Elysian consciousness, but he seemed to relish the delay between the idea and its notation.

He didn't feel betrayed anymore. He felt wiser and therefore grateful. Death allowed him to keep his distance. Over and over, he'd attempted to explain his absence in letters, but he never mailed them because doing so would break the vow he'd taken. The bequest he was about to make might not redeem him, but it enabled him to show up without showing up.

What was in it for him? Speculation abounds about the motivation underlying his machinations. Some ascribe them to paternal love tormented and poisoned by lingering resentment toward his own father figure—Abdullah Ibn Buhaina, more commonly known as Art Blakey, the bebop drummer and bandleader rumored to have deliberately addicted young sidemen in order to exercise control over them. Others say the fateful consequences of his actions make the psychodrama irrelevant. Was he a moral visionary or a nihilist prankster? In the final analysis, he was an artist, a sculptor of dead souls.

A single sheet of music would say all that had to be said, without the degradation of words. Music has to be interpreted. That's what makes it communication.

Had Lee trained as an avant-garde composer, maybe he would have aimed a shotgun at a blank score and blasted the notes with one pull of the trigger. As it was, he used a lead pencil rather than lead buckshot, but the melody was incised just as forcefully. Blood leaked from the punctures in the page.

Touching pencil point to the top of the sheet, he then printed the words: *Paternal Lee.*

✖

Effortlessly, he rose in rank, becoming Coltrane's most favored disciple by subjugating his own ego to serve the vision of a master who yearned to shake off the yoke of King Charlie and Queen Billie. Revered, if not universally beloved, Bird and Lady Day encouraged improvisation, but only within a strict framework. Carefully managed freedom would never spill over into anarchy. The appointment of renegade saxophonist Albert Ayler to the island's highest ecclesiastical office represented a calculated bid on their part to give symbolic voice to wild impulses without investing them with any true power.

No title at all was bestowed upon Eric Dolphy, who was rarely seen except at dusk, skulking along the shores of Jazz Island fingering an invisible horn. In peacetime no use could be found for his mad genius.

The cloak of chief minister chafed Coltrane's skin. His spiritual aura concealed a burning ambition. Only the disciple could readily detect it, perhaps because he too craved power.

"If something happened that grabbed the populace by the throat," he hypothesized. "A scandal, a controversy. Something that forced everyone to take sides. A declaration of war."

"That would violate our national commitment toward reason and reflection," Coltrane countered. "The prosperity of Jazz Island rests on fairness."

"Ultimately, yes, fairness will be restored. We can rely on the orderly nature of Jazz Island reasserting itself afterwards."

"After what?"

✖

Fortuitously, the trumpeter overheard Lady Day discussing the potential military threat posed by Hiphopabad.

Lady Day may be a lot of things, Bird liked to say, but she ain't no lady. Elegance and poise belied a rancid heart. She had lived for money, drugs, sex, and violence; convinced that everyone wanted what she wanted and wanted what she had, she had never let her guard down for a second. None of these existed in the Flipside. The only thing left was power, but that was enough for her. Bessie Smith and Dinah Washington, the only other vocalists she countenanced, served as attendants in her court and tried to moderate her aggressive tendencies, but most times merely inflamed them.

Game recognized game, and in Tupac Amaru Shakur she saw a mirror reflection of her own ruthless grace. It was only a matter of time before they crossed swords, and here in the Flipside, the inevitable showdown had already begun.

It wasn't the militancy of Hiphopabad that alarmed Coltrane. "It's those DJs I worry about."

"They spin records on turntables," the king said. "Am I right? Sometimes the records get scratched, which is unfortunate."

"But it's got nothing to do with us," the queen responded.

"They're stealing our music," Coltrane insisted. "And, what's worse, making new music out of it."

"As you did with 'Summertime' and 'My Favorite Things.'"

"I took liberties with those songs, it's true, but there was never any question that the melodies belonged to George Gershwin and Richard Rogers. As a matter of fact, George and I have discussed this matter, and he agrees with me. On the other hand, when audiences today hear *this…*" [he paused to play "Skylark"], "they no longer have any idea it's Hoagy Carmichael's tune; they're bobbing their heads to Mobb Deep."

"Jazz is immortal," smiled the queen. "Weren't we worried about rock and roll and rhythm and blues?"

"This is different. They don't want to conquer us. They want to usurp us."

Bird and Holiday weren't especially alarmed, but they respected Coltrane enough to consent to his proposal to gather intelligence regarding Hiphopabad's true intentions. They selected Clifford Brown for the mission.

✷

Lee folded the sheet into thirds with exact creases and inserted it into an album sleeve carefully designed to capture Jay's interest. He'd commissioned a graphic artist to fabricate it in the style of Polydor covers from the label's mid-seventies heyday. Everything was fake, from artist and title to track listing and personnel, but *Shady Business* by Beulah and the Beauts would leap from a stuffed crate into the DJ's greedy fingers with no hesitation. It wasn't necessary to fabricate a record. The disk inside was one by Roy Ayers Ubiquity that would certainly be in Jay's vast collection already, but by the time he realized that, the composition would have possessed him.

✷

Brown's report on Hiphopabad described an alien culture where explosions reverberated throughout the night. Doge Tupac and General Eazy-E reveled in the noise, content that their borders were expanding like spilled wine soaking into a silk tablecloth. At all-night banquets in Thugz Mansion, Tupac proclaimed victory after victory, praising the ferocity of his generals and promising remorseless evisceration of all haters.

"It isn't enough to wound," he declared. "It isn't enough to kill. We don't settle for mere murder and mayhem. It's got to be a motherfucking massacre that would make your grandchildren's grandchildren hang their heads in shame. War crimes! Ethnic motherfucking cleansing!"

Brown's memo then revealed another layer of intrigue:

```
Unbeknownst to the doge and his ministers,
the detonations are only samples - recordings
cleverly designed to sound concussive within
the banquet hall. Co-led by DJ Screw and
J Dilla, the tribe of sonic counterfeiters
are motivated less by treason and more by
hatred of carnage. As they see it, the city-
state has attained a manageable and healthy
equilibrium, which unnecessary conflict would
only destabilize.

     New generations of bloodthirsty emcees
continue to join the fray. Hotheaded and
reckless, they vow to kill and maim each and
every hater living in the jealous nations that
surround them.

     Gunfire echoes within the walls of the
city-state day and night, but the truth is,
the military threat is minimal. Nobody dies.
Sure, they die, but they don't stay dead. They
go out pyrotechnically, each with a unique
soundtrack that outdoes previous Hiphopabad
deaths, and then they come back in much the
same form as before. It is eternal and ever
more spectacular, a kind of video game Kabuki.
When Pop Smoke, Nipsey Hussle, Juice WRLD,
or any of the lesser lights step to an Ol'
```

Dirty Bastard or Big Pun, the firestorms can
be blinding, with guts and brains everywhere,
but when the dust settles, the status quo
prevails.

In conclusion, as long as we and the other
republics continue to comport ourselves as
peaceful neighbors – alert to the bellicosity
of Hiphopabad but not concerned enough to
respond militarily to sound effects – the
peace should hold.

✖

Gracefully, the trumpeter would insinuate his musical legacy
into the sensibility of the next generation. And was there
in fact a biological connection? In 1964, the year his breakthrough hit "The Sidewinder" was released, did he happen
perchance to sire Jason Mizell—the boy who would become
Jam Master Jay?

We'll never know. Jazz isn't immortal, but genius is. The
body it inhabits might fail too soon—this happens all the
time—but the incandescent spirit migrates fulfills its promise
out of earshot. It has nothing to do with earthly memory or
artistic influence. Mizell came into the world on January 21,
1965. Everybody said he looked like his mother. He started
playing trumpet at age three, eventually switching to drums
before discovering—largely inventing, one could say—the
two-turntable DJ kit.

People claimed he could drop the needle at the exact perfect break, just by looking at the vinyl. That's a lie. He could
have done it blindfolded. Just as pupils—the little black holes
at the center of the iris—are sensitive to light, his fingertips
felt the sound in the groove.

The search for records further illuminated Jay's genius.
Digging through crates at the Flipside transported him to
an alternate time flow, neither faster nor slower than the

standard clock but more logical and crystalline. Under the streets of Times Square, the world receded into heavy smog as independently intelligent fingers rifled through the albums, absorbing thousands upon thousands of studio hours via an exquisite sense of touch. Each album he touched triggered lightning-fast calculations that couldn't be put into words, the population and calibration of a multidimensional database of sound, subculture, and story.

If Charlie Parker had killed composition so music could live, Jay had slain improvisation, virtuosity. Make no mistake, Jay had the chops, just as Parker could compose, but that was no longer enough. The future belonged to instinct, a more dangerous—even explosive—power. He paused every so often to glance at a back cover, but less than one in a thousand titles made it into his satchel.

Before Jay played a new record, a vacuum would fill his ears, a sound-shaped ache. Just before inevitable disappointment set in, he had a fleeting taste of what he sought. It wasn't delicious. It was inexorable, like the vinyl circling the hole clockwise, like bloody water disappearing down a drain.

What made the cut? More to the point, what was he looking for? To say he was a DJ—and crate-digging is what DJs do—would miss what made Jay the pre-eminent DJ of hip-hop's golden era. He searched not to find something but because he felt most whole while searching.

Still, searching for *what*? Inside Jay gaped a hole, a black hole that could never be filled. Or hadn't yet. Maybe someday a previously unknown album (a circle with a hole in the middle) would plug that hole once and for all.

Only one thing would fill the hole, and it's a thing that itself had a hole, which cried out to be filled with a thing that— you guessed it—had a hole in the middle. And on and on, until the succession of holes formed a tunnel, a groove that both filled and could not ever be filled. The emptiness inside

Jay grew vaster the more he filled it. His drug addiction, like Lee's, was another hole that couldn't be filled.

What put the hole there in the first place—or what *didn't* take place that gave rise to the black hole? These are the questions.

The moment came when he held the Beauts album by its edges. There had been countless such moments in his past, moments that held the possibility—or perhaps the impossibility—of a cure for the sickness that had afflicted him all his life. This wasn't medicine, it was faith healing—that is, healing that relied on belief. Belief in something that couldn't be seen or heard, that probably wasn't there. But maybe! The *maybe* was reason enough.

Opening the folded sheet that had drifted out of the record cover, Jay immediately started reading quarter notes and eighth notes—black circles on a grooved background that perfectly fit the holes inside him. He kept the melody within him until the day he died full of bullet holes. And beyond.

✖

During their lives both Lee and Jay had poisoned their bloodstreams. In the Flipside, the tainted hemorrhage came out as pure music. The notation was not the song. It was the sperm, the pollen. A song can't blossom without it, but inspiration alone is merely eye irritant.

To become a truly great song, the inspiration must penetrate another consciousness. We could call that the egg, but the metaphor can only stretch so far. Creative artists have impregnated themselves and subsequently hatched fully formed songs, but no matter how ingenious they are, they tend to be insular, wan, lacking in vitality.

Jay was more than a musician. Like Lee, he was a recombinator. Through rapid-fire reweaving of musical bloodlines, each of them accelerated musical evolution at many times the natural rate.

There have been tens of millions of songs, but just a few dozen have entered the pantheon. It happens mysteriously, but when it does, it's undeniable. "Amazing Grace" is one. "Danny Boy," "Summertime," "Unchained Melody," "My Way," "Let It Be Me." Thanks to Coltrane, "My Favorite Things" made it. The 1960s were a particularly fertile period, beginning with "Will You Love Me Tomorrow," and continuing with "Yesterday," "People Get Ready," "Everybody's Talkin'," "Gentle on My Mind," and "Wichita Lineman," all of them love songs, the only kind that are worth the breath. Once all the songs that compose the universe had been discovered, some experts have contended, there could be no more. Their ultimate number is fixed, like the number of bones in a human skeleton; it's a natural law, or was believed to be. "Paternal Lee" shattered these certainties. One analyst compared it to finding a 65th square on the checkerboard. It shouldn't exist, but there it is.

✖

Actually, Brown's memorandum had neglected to disclose one key aspect of DJ culture. Like his playing, his lean prose omitted volumes, but he'd nevertheless witnessed how the competitive spirit in Hiphopabad rested on a shared aspiration toward excellence. While DJs jealously guarded some of their technical secrets, a culture of mentorship and camaraderie predominated. Everybody accorded elders such as DJ Scott La Rock and Jam Master Jay the utmost respect. When a new DJ or producer arrived—a rare occurrence, given their comparatively risk-averse conduct in the earthly realm—he treated his forebears with deference, eager to gain access to the tips and tricks they were willing to reveal. Coltrane University could learn a thing or two from Hiphopabad, he thought to himself.

What's more, it turned out that for many years Dolphy and other disgruntled jazz artists had been visiting the

basement of Thugz Mansion to participate in bold experi-
ments. When Brown first encountered a jam session in progress there, he barely recognized the music as music, but as
he lingered through the night, he caught on to the subtle
textures.

"What's the point of all this?" he asked DJ Scott La Rock.

"This is pure science. You should sit in."

"What's the plan, though? Are you going on the
offensive?"

"No, man. In a world of speakers, we're the listeners. But
that doesn't mean we're passive."

Dolphy approached, putting a hand on Brown's shoulder. "We're making real progress, but things are still at a very
preliminary stage. We don't want too much attention yet, if
you follow."

✖

Brown's dispatch placated Coltrane, but Lady Day was un-
convinced and grew increasingly ill at ease. She cared little
for a sideman's admiration of Hiphopabad's secondary culture and insisted on detailed accounts of Tupac's behavior
and declarations, no matter how buffoonish or impractical.
(What about the Notorious B.I.G.? you ask. Didn't he reside
in Hiphopabad, too? Well, that's another story.)

She asked Coltrane to send another emissary. "Someone
willing to get his hands dirty. Not one of these aesthetic prima
donnas. Get me a junkie, someone who's taken a bullet. We
need a bastard."

"What you seem to be saying," Bessie Smith ventured,
"is that you're basically okay with unreliable."

"I'm basically okay with a motherfucker."

✖

Lee Morgan marched into the DJ lair, his trumpet to his
mouth, and joined the ensemble without waiting for an

invitation. Chick Webb hunched over the drum kit, with Charlie Christian and Scott La Faro rounding out the rhythm section. The eternally 28-year-old cornetist Bix Beiderbecke (b. 1903) dueled and duetted with the eternally 32-year-old J. Dilla (b. 1974) on his Akai MPC3000. Spanning generations and genres, this all-star combo sculpted a new sound. The music was not futuristic; it was beyond history entirely, a cacophonous hush slipping in and out of an irreducible time signature, a contradictory key. It continually wound down, further and further, without ever ending.

Jam Master Jay was positioned nearby, absorbing the groove without participating until Morgan made his entrance. He had never heard "Paternal Lee" out loud, and the recognition staggered him for a moment.

Jay dropped two platters on his decks, reached over and unplugged Dilla's setup without asking permission, and revved up a sonic landscape that enveloped the jazzmen. Soon the subterranean air filled with a duet between trumpeter and DJ, a painful pointillistic cascade with a syncopated line that swung like a scythe.

Big Pun, all 700 pounds of him, pounced on the mic. "This is the new weapon we warned you about," he hollered, but Dolphy's horn broke in with an irrefutable counterpoint: *Weapon? It's the opposite. This is a religion, a new era with no use for weapons. This is what 'A Love Supreme' pretended to be.*

Jay nodded at Lee and then beckoned to someone in the shadows. DJ Screw brought out a vintage microphone, and Queen Billie took center stage, tapping her black pump to a rhythm only two others in the lair could hear. Her legendary warble wrapped itself around seemingly improvised lyrics: "What did I know, what did I know, of love's austere and lonely offices?"

The unfamiliar-familiar music wafted up to Tupac's tower chamber, and he calmly loaded two semiautomatic rifles before descending to the depths. "Paternal Lee" rang in his ears as he stood in the subterranean doorway, awaiting a signal from within. Altered ineffably by his presence, the jam proceeded at a slightly slower tempo, acquiring a noirishly suspenseful but also somewhat mocking undercurrent.

With characteristic languor, Billie turned her face to the doorway and greeted her nemesis with a bittersweet glance during a pause between verses.

Drawing his weapons with a flourish that he knew looked cinematic, even though it actually delayed the pulling of triggers, the Doge of Hiphopabad roared silently as the spray of bullets became a whirlwind of gardenias and doves, while the performers remained upright and continued to play, egged on by the gunfire percussion to a sprightly doubletime break.

Limb by limb, Tupac's anatomy became weaponry, discharging and clattering to the floor while the music carried on, now a victorious jubilee, now an old-world waltz. When the smoke cleared, the Queen was gone, but the funnel of petals and feathers swirled eternally.

✱

And thus arose the joint kingdom of New Syncopia. King Charlie Parker raised no objections to the new regime but felt compelled to abdicate, while Coltrane insisted that Lee Morgan's continued presence at court would destabilize the delicate alliance. "Motherfuckers like that just can't tolerate normality," he argued. "He's incapable of leaving well enough alone." ODB concurred, declaring somewhat disingenuously that spiritual growth depended on political harmony.

King Jay then ascended the throne, while Lee took to roaming the outskirts of the Flipside, eventually disappearing into legend.

WAITING FOR THE SON

The future's uncertain and the end is always near
—The Doors, "Roadhouse Blues"

See the sunlight, we ain't stoppin'
Keep on dancin' 'til the world ends
—Britney Spears, "Till the World Ends"

WAITING FOR THE SON

Compliance associate at a fintech startup was my first real job since graduating from Sarah Lawrence with a degree in American Studies. I hadn't yet figured out quite what the company did or what laws we were or weren't compliant with, but it paid way better than digitizing the archives of the NYC Department of Health and Mental Hygiene, and the CEO treated everyone decently. He may have been some kind of financial genius, but as a person he would have been completely unexceptional if it hadn't been for one quirk—the dubious conviction that he was Jim Morrison's love child. Evidently his mother had lived in Paris in the early 1970s and spent time with the rock star during his final days.

The main conference room was called the Soul Kitchen. Receptionists answered the phone with "Hello, I love you, won't you tell me your name?" When we got stuck on a compliance issue, we were urged to "break on through to the other side" of whatever the problem was. If the half-billion-dollar initial public offering was any indication, investors weren't too worried about our problems.

My first and best work friend knew even less about financial technology than I did, but Geena was far better at figuring out how to endear herself. Which was why HR had entrusted us with flying to Vegas for RockMusiCon in search of Doors memorabilia to give to the boss on his thirty-fourth birthday.

"Rock and roll," I said, "seems to excite the most boring people on the planet."

"Hasn't every girl our age dated at least one Beatlemaniac?"

The Beatlemaniac remark put me in mind of an old almost-flame. Todd and I were friends throughout high school until he tried kissing me at a graduation party. I told him it felt like being hit in the face with a baseball bat, and he got pouty, but over the years I wondered if maybe I shouldn't have let him slip away. He made me sculptures out of Gummy Bears and toothpicks. Todd didn't actually like the Beatles ("too much signal, not enough noise"), but he had Lennon's aquiline nose and insolent mouth.

Just before I moved to New York, Todd was killed by his mentally ill younger brother, and ever since, Lennon's voice and face have evoked Todd in my heart—a quarter-sized mass that always radiated heat and sometimes glowed red hot, singeing the surrounding tissue.

✖

The event left us empty-handed and restless. None of the bootlegs or memorabilia on offer seemed special enough for our purpose, and the vendors and collectors alike creeped us out. The body odor of past conventioneers emanated in waves from the exhibition hall carpet.

Back in our hotel room, Geena was munching on popcorn and watching *Blue Crush* while flipping through the inch-thick hotel magazine. I looked out the window just as a topless peroxide blonde popped out of the sunroof of a stretch limousine. *Thinks she's having fun but she's someone else's plaything. Thinks she's the object of envy but she's mostly ignored. Thinks she's special but she's totally replaceable. Thinks nobody sees how miserable she is but that's all anybody who bothered to look would see.* It was like looking into a cruelly accurate mirror.

Interrupting my reverie, Geena called out, "Does this sound good to you: 'Live crucifixion—accepting volunteers.' Or we could go see a band called Abortiodontist. And look, Dara! Tonya Harding recites *Moby Dick*!" She slurped the last of her Manhattan. "Just kidding. She mud-wrestles a dwarf."

"Let's just order sundaes," I said, "and drop Maraschino cherries out the window on people down below."

"Or," Geena answered, "We could go see *Riders of the Storm*." She read aloud: "Experience Jim Morrison and the Doors just as they were the night they played the Vegas Ice Palace in October 1969."

"Why not, I guess?"

✖

The over-air-conditioned hall, half-filled with comped locals and befuddled Dutch tourists, felt like a retired Disney attraction. A paunchy man in a tan uniform, Stetson hat, and mirrored sunglasses emerged from behind a red velvet curtain. "Ladies and gentlemen!" he began, "I am Sheriff Ralph Lamb, patriot and churchgoing lawman [*scattered hisses*], and I am deeply disgusted by each and every one of you for daring to come into our happy and healthy community to witness this obscene spectacle tonight! [*Rising mutters*] So-called singer James Morrison is a known pervert and drug addict. [*Applause, punctuated by hoots of approval*] Wherever he and his hippie followers go, the result is the same. Teenagers smoking marijuana—and much, much worse! [*Cheers*] Vandalizing property! [*Louder cheers*] Rioting, raping, and ruining instead of reading, writing, and 'rithmetic! [*Laughter and shrieks of delight*] Simmer down, you reprobates! A group of concerned citizens petitioned the Clark County District Attorney to ban this vile exhibition from our fair city, but he maintains that the Doors have a First Amendment right to perform. So I have no choice but to introduce to you the corrupt, the filthy, the LEGENDARY Doors! [*Rapturous acclaim as the sheriff pulls open the front of his uniform to reveal a Jim Morrison t-shirt.*]

The lewd, bluesy organ crunch of "Touch Me" began, the curtain lifted, and we all played the part of rabid Doors fans. The effect was more convincing if you didn't look too hard at the band members, especially the elderly Black woman on keyboards. But the singer was plausibly Morrisonian, a couple of years out of high school, at most, and blessed with the requisite moves and physique, as well as the pipes. The finale of "Light My Fire" went on at least three times too long, but the sight of stage flames licking his shiny torso held our interest.

Geena effortlessly hustled us backstage afterwards. "Where did you learn all that?" she asked the sweat-soaked front man.

Any resemblance to Morrison vanished under the glare of the dressing-room bulbs. Rather than an unearthly pallor, he had a deep tan, or perhaps a south-of-the-border grandparent or two. And there was no profundity in his gaze, only perplexity.

"Videos, mostly. I've watched the Val Kilmer movie like a hundred times."

"How long have you been performing here?"

"I guess it's been seven months now."

Geena tugged on his hair. It stayed on. "What's your real name, Jim?"

"Alfonso, ma'am."

"Alfonso, if you call me ma'am again I'm going to have to ravish you something fierce."

"Were you already a Doors fan, Alfonso?" I asked.

"That's the thing," he said. "I hadn't even heard of them.

Then one night around two in the morning, I'm installing barbed-wire fence around a campground when this old Buick pulls up and two guys come over and start talking to me."

"Wait, why were you installing a fence in the middle of the night?"

"I guess you've never dug holes on a hot day in Nevada."

"Ah. So what did the guys say to you? How did they even know you had any talent?"

"They said someone showed them video of me onstage with my rap group, but honestly, I think it was more about how my jeans fit. They were like, Can we take your picture? I'm like, Okay but I'm not doing anything perverted. They're like, We'll give you a hundred dollars to move around like you're the Lizard King."

"And then?"

"I guess I moved around okay, shaking my shoulders and swishing my imaginary tail around. And then they're like, There's someone we want you to meet. I say, What about the fence? and they're like, Forget about the fence, and they take me to this motel room where there's this old guy, really fat, not so healthy. They tell me he knew Jim Morrison personally. Like they were best friends or something, practically brothers. And they leave me alone with him. It's kinda dark, but I can see he's not wearing any clothes . . . not that he tries anything, though."

"What *did* he do?"

"We just talked."

"What did he say?"

"He's like, Are you ready to sing the blues? And I'm like, I don't know, man, what are the blues? And he struggles to stand up on the bed, butt naked, like he's a bear trying to do gymnastics, and starts going, *Yeah, yeah, yeah,* and then *Ow, ow, ow,* like someone's whipping his back. Which kind of freaks me out, because I'm thinking someone's going to bust in and accuse me of elder abuse."

"Then what?"

"The two guys come back, and they're like, what are you doing Friday night? And I'm like, Nothing. So I've been doing this show ever since, five nights a week. The songs are nothing like the hip-hop I used to do, but they're pretty cool, and the people seem to really like me."

"Anything weird ever happen?"

"Weird how? Are you cops?"

"She's just, like, *into* weird," Geena laughed. "Is that a problem?"

"No, ma'am. I mean, no. But a lot of people who come here seem to be on LSD for the first time, or the first time in a long time. Some of them don't handle it too well. The crew have a lot to mop up."

"Did you ever see the blues guy again?"

"Actually, he came by just a week ago and told me Jim would have liked the show. And he handed me a copy of that biography, *No One Here Gets Out Alive*. It was all beat up, with stuff crossed out and writing all over the pages."

"You still have it?"

"Nah. Turns out it was an overdue library book, so I returned it."

"There's a *library* here?"

"Sure, it's like any other place. We have a fire department and ice cream parlors and public swimming pools and everything. There's way more to Vegas than strippers and the strip, you know."

✖

The next morning, instead of flying back to New York, we pushed our flight back a day, rented a convertible, and set out to search Las Vegas's libraries. Geena called shotgun. Our universe shrank to a single dimension as we slid back and forth along the boom and bust of this parody of the American Dream. The sun scorched our retinas while the radio played nothing but indistinguishable boy bands and Britney Spears, whose voice brought to mind the topless girl popping out of the sunroof on the Strip. I shuttled us from one end of the strip to the other, entered a circular drive, and swung back around in the opposite direction again. It gave me time to think, but nothing to think about.

Three hours later, we had visited five public libraries but failed to discover a marked-up copy of *No One Here Gets Out Alive*. It was the hottest part of the day, and I wanted to abandon the car and wander away forever, but Geena convinced me to go shopping for leather pants instead. She took the wheel and changed the station to Classic Rock. The song about a desert highway was our song, she cooed.

As we were heading toward the outlet stores, she suddenly swerved into yet another strip mall. "Dara!" she exclaimed, "How did we miss this one?" She pulled up in front of a low structure resembling an abandoned liquor store, complete with barred windows and glass splinters twinkling on the parking-lot asphalt. The church-style letters on the sign out front read SIN CITY MUNICIPAL MUSIC LIB'ARY.

A German shepherd chained to an overflowing dumpster completed the junkyard aesthetic, but the rows of shelving on the other side of the screen door, if not quite parallel, did indeed hold reading material. Ceiling tiles buckled above a lopsided metal counter stacked high with LPs, back issues of music magazines, and, for some reason, carpet samples. The smell of moldering newsprint and low-calorie beer hung in the air like an inappropriate joke.

A wire-spectacled figure in a red pajama top and tight white satin bell-bottoms acknowledged us from the stacks but made no motion to approach the counter. The guitar solo from "Hotel California" snaked out of his transistor radio, presumably tuned to the same station as our car stereo, though the tinny speaker made it sound like a cover version.

"We're looking for a book by a musician," I announced.

"Then you're in luck," the Librarian replied. "We have both kinds here, rock *and* roll." His faint British accent gave the gloom a slightly more inviting glimmer. His pajama top was mostly unbuttoned, revealing a thick gold braid amid a carpet of silver chest hair. A not-so-innocent grin lurked beneath his baggy eyes and bulbous nose.

"Actually," I said, "We're looking for a specific copy of the Jim Morrison biography, one that was returned about a week ago."

He nodded and disappeared behind a freestanding room divider. While we waited, I noticed a rusting file cabinet with LAZ. stenciled on the front and began inching my way toward it, but the Librarian re-emerged before I could reach for a handle.

"*So* sorry. That copy is not currently in circulation."

"Do you know when will it be back in circulation?"

"Perhaps you should come back tomorrow," he smiled. "In the meantime, I have quite an extensive collection of memorabilia here, if you tell me what your interest is."

"Rock stars," I said. "Dead ones."

He fixed me with a knowing gaze. "I may have just the thing," he said. "It's a recent acquisition, and I don't know whether to classify it as fiction or nonfiction. We get all kinds of donations from all kinds of sources, and I've learned not to ask too many questions." He slid open the LAZ. drawer, pulled out a butterfly-clip-bound packet, and placed it on the counter in front of us. "You might learn a thing or two."

Accompanied by the opening guitar line of "Stairway to Heaven," we thanked him and promised to return the next day.

"Freaky old hippy," I laughed on the way out.

"I don't know," Geena answered slowly. "The way he looked at me, it was kind of…"

"Satanic?"

✖

We pushed back our flights again and returned to the Sin City Lib'ary just before noon the next day to find the Librarian talking to a woman with caked-on makeup and a mop of ash-blonde hair. He was in full flow.

"Sam Cooke with 'A Change Is Gonna Come' and Otis Redding with 'Dock of the Bay'—that's how to make an exit in style. And Johnny Ace's "Pledging My Love" is the greatest swan song of all time, of course, not just because of the Russian roulette. Do you know what a swan song is?"

"It's the name of Led Zeppelin's label."

"Very good, but do you know the myth behind it? The ancients believed a swan only sings just before it dies, when the most beautiful song emerges from its graceful throat. That's what Sam and Otis managed."

"'It's better to burn out,'" quoted his companion, "'than to fade away.'"

"Very good. When people tell me all the great rock stars died young, I like to point out all the ones who *didn't* die when perhaps they should have. Now if Elvis Presley had left the building in 1969 after singing Bacharach and Hilliard's 'Any Day Now'"—here the Librarian paused to intone—"'Until you've gone forever, I'll be holding on for dear life, holding you this way, begging you to stay," he'd have spared us all that seventies dreck. Same with Eric Clapton and 'Layla' or Lou Reed and 'Sweet Jane.' They'd have left elegant corpses behind and the airwaves would have never been polluted by 'I Shot the Sheriff' or 'Walk on the Wild Side.'

"Diana Ross could have ended on a gorgeous Ashford and Simpson high note with 'Remember Me'; her self-indulgent Billie Holiday tribute would have remained an exquisitely unrealized ambition. Whereas look at the overfed, overweening zombies we're stuck with: Brian Wilson, the Eagles, and, no offense, Stevie Wonder selling out the lawn on their third farewell tours. And don't get me started on Van Morrison or Rod Stewart."

"Van the Flan! Rod the Cod!"

"Double bingo, kid."

"Have I told you lately that I drugged you?" She batted her lashes in exaggerated fashion.

"They denied us the deities we crave because they had the gall to outstay their welcome."

He paused and looked up at us, seemingly unable to recall where he had seen us before, but it hit him before we had to say anything. He scurried off, leaving us with the blonde.

"You're in a band, aren't you?" asked Geena.

"Kind of," she said, averting her eyes.

"What are you called?"

"You probably haven't heard of us."

"Wait, aren't you in Abortiodontist? I think I saw your picture in the hotel magazine."

"Here you go," the Librarian said, waving a worn paperback in the air. "The Jim Morrison biography, complete with a rare postscript. Unverified, of course."

"How unverified?"

"Stop me if you've heard this before," he said, winking at his friend. "I don't know, and I don't care. There's a lot of stuff here that's been entrusted to me. I've been asked to hold onto it. I'm not given certificates of authenticity. Some of it might be valuable, and some of it is probably bogus. Maybe it's all bogus. All I can say is, this *might* be the volume you requested."

✖

The library copy of *No One Here Gets Out Alive* was a mess. Several photos had been exed out. Quotes had been amended. Exclamation points sprouted everywhere. One entire chapter had been ripped out. My eyes strained to decipher the cramped handwriting of the comments that littered the margins and the

"postscript" that filled the previously blank pages in the back
of the book, which seemed to be some kind of parable.

He was a preacher of great renown, adored by
hordes of teenage worshippers and feared by
the rearguard. Both sides wondered about the
sincerity of his ardor and recognized the risk
of his cult cresting. He alone knew he was a
fraud and, regrettably, no cause for alarm.

Then late one night he ducked into the
Orpheum and caught a biker flick. The onscreen
action meant nothing to him, but the power of
the medium lit a fire beneath his stomach. He
didn't want to be a movie star, for he had
already had his fill of mindless adulation. It
was the original American tale: He needed to
start again as someone else. To give birth to
the movies in his mind, he had to vanish from
the pulpit and reappear somewhere new, with
new clothes and a new name.

The craft of cinema might as well have
been inorganic chemistry, so obscured was it
from his ken. It would come. And besides, a
sufficient portion of the gold he'd amassed
as a preacher remained in his possession. The
acquisition of equipment and personnel was a
simple matter. What he needed was a story —
the story. Millions couldn't buy that.

The preacher ascended the highest peak in
the land and found nothing there. He made a
home in the ghetto and found nothing there.
But then he moved to the Mississippi Delta,
and there discovered his cinematic muse.

(And killed her.)

Folded in quarters and scotch-taped to the inside cover of the book were two sheets of goldenrod mimeograph paper. The first was professionally designed (though with no great skill).

FLICKS THAT STICK TO YOUR "SOUL"
Orpheum Floor Pictures | Mail Order

- ❏ COVER GIRLS UNDERCOVER (1972, 70 min.)
  A blonde, a redhead, and an oriental from a high-class fashion model agency infiltrate an organized crime ring pushing a dangerous new drug on the streets of New Orleans.

- ❏ BAYOU HONEY (1972, 82 min.)
  Growing up in the swamps of Louisiana, Lily Mae learned to do two things very well: play the fiddle and shoot a rifle. She's going to need both skills when she goes after the men that killed her daddy.

- ❏ THE BLOODY TUNNEL (1973, 75 min.)
  After a prison guard and a convicted murderer discover they're twins, they break all the rules in pursuit of a buried treasure.

- ❏ THE BLOODY CAVERN (1973, 90 min.)
  Identical twins Luke and Duke Norris join forces again for a big score, but things get complicated when they fall in love with the same cat burglar.

Order today. $9.95 each, or all four for $29.95.
Orpheum Floor Pictures,13795 Airline Hwy Box 991, Baton Rouge, La. 70817.

The second contained a brief statement punched out on a mid-century typewriter:

Eisenhower won the war so he could become president so he could build the highways so I could stand at the side of the road with my

```
thumb out. All prehistory and history build
to this very moment when you pull over, roll
down the window, and ask how far I'm going.
'Riders' isn't a song. It's an epic crying
out for celluloid. It might take a thousand
takes before I get it right. The film in the
camera, the blood in my veins and the cars on
the road all flow onward. They make the clock
tick. They make the earth spin on its axis. I
never felt time when I stood before the masses
delivering the gospel. I was a drunken ape,
staggering without purpose.
```

✖

Convinced that it would mean promotions for both of us, Geena persuaded me to bring the library copy and inserts back with us from Vegas and present them to the boss.

Within a week, he had disappeared, along with $521 million, and I went back to the Health and Human Hygiene archives. Geena and I met for drinks a few times, but eventually our shared Vegas memories lost their sparkle.

About a year later, a package arrived from Baton Rouge. Inside was a DVD:

LOVE PYRAMID
A father, a son, and the Egyptian goddess
they're both in love with.

THE SOUND N FURY DEMOS

For Ron Rosenbaum

THE SOUND N FURY DEMOS

North of the Okefenokee Swamp and south of Waycross, Georgia, a banker's-box-sized cube of speckled pink granite squats in the crabgrass between the lanes of Jacksonville Highway. On a chilly October morning in 1983, two men meet here at dawn, as they do every year on this date. This is the first time they've allowed anybody else, let alone a journalist, to join them.

"Hello, William."

"Good morning, Governor. Can you believe another year has gone by?"

Dressed in a somber three-piece suit, James Earl Carter Jr, known to all as Jimmy, falls to his knees and brushes gravel and sticks off the granite marker. Denim-clad William Grace makes the sign of the cross as Jimmy rises and the morning light allows the name chiseled on the stone to become legible: VERONICA.

"She'd be thirteen years old now," Jimmy says.

"Ready for high school, just about," Grace replies.

"She was a beautiful girl. It was a terrible night."

"Terrible for all of us, Governor, but in particular for you. You were on your way to the White House."

"I don't think about it that way," Jimmy says, squinting. "Not anymore."

"You were ahead in the polls. You would have made a fine president."

"You know I don't like to dwell on something that wasn't in God's plan."

William Grace, who once wrote a smash-hit show unique in the annals of American musical theater—and who, some people still insist, used to be a rock star who went by the name Gram Parsons—looks away. "I was a great sinner," he states. "My sins had sins growing on their backs."

Jimmy barely suppresses an eye roll. "You persist in bragging on your sins. It's a way of running from the pain. From the truth. From the Lord."

"Now I'm washed in the blood of the Lamb. My heart is pure."

"Not too pure, I hope. The purest hearts scare me the most. With nothing to resist, the muscle withers."

To Jimmy's evident consternation, Grace lights a cigarette. "I feel so old, Governor. The years are eating holes in me."

"I believe I have a couple decades on you."

"Sometimes I wake up," Grace continues. "Planning everything that has to get done for the performance that night. What's my role? Are the band and cast ready? What about the props? And then I remember everything has become foreign, faded. False."

"Let's both pray on that," Jimmy says as a Volkswagen pulls up alongside them. "See you next year," he adds and climbs in with barely a wave. The car is driven by a woman in an ornate hat and veil who I presume is his wife, Rosalyn, although she strongly brings to mind the woman in Lefty Frizzell's classic "The Long Black Veil."

✖

This is a tale of two very different Georgians inextricably linked by catastrophe. Jimmy Carter, the Democratic presidential candidate who lost to incumbent Gerald Ford in 1976, may warrant a brief mention in the history books, but today he is largely forgotten. William Grace has almost completely vanished from the public memory, but to know him, you first have to know who he says he *isn't*: Gram Parsons, the singer-songwriter-star who officially died at age 26 on September 19, 1973, in Room 8 of the Joshua Tree Inn in Joshua Tree, California. Parsons had a successful solo career as well as a stint with the Byrds. He was a heavy drinker and partier who turned Keith Richards on to country music, inspiring "Wild Horses"—which he recorded before the Stones themselves did so. According to most accounts, a roadie stole Gram's body just before it was to be shipped to Louisiana for burial, drove it back to Joshua Tree in a borrowed hearse, and attempted to cremate it using five gallons of gasoline before the authorities recovered the remains.

✖

In a diner not far from the roadside marker, Grace looks wounded when I point out that nearby Waycross is Gram Parsons's hometown. "It was the All-Night Sing that brought me here," he says, referring to a Shriners-sponsored traditional event that attracts gospel music aficionados from all over the world.

Unlike Parsons, who inhaled liquor and drugs and favored elaborately festive suits tailor-made by Nuta Kotlyarenko (known professionally as Nudie Cohn), Grace drinks nothing stronger than Celestial Seasonings tea this morning and is dressed modestly in mismatched denim. A gray-speckled brush cut gives a radically different impression than the David Cassidy do sported by Parsons in his prime.

Extensive public and private inquiries seem to confirm that the charred remains recovered in Joshua Tree were those of Parsons. Grace acknowledges that he bears a superficial resemblance to the singer but declines to say anything further about the rumors that have swirled around him for years. Nor will he provide any documentation of his past, saying only that he's a native Georgian who is not in touch with his family. "All I ask," he says, "is to have nothing to do with those people ever again."

Grace slides out of the booth, leaving me with the check—and a Memorex cassette he pulled from his shirt pocket. *S&F* is written on the label in blue ballpoint.

✖

Whoever he is, there is no doubt that Grace wrote, produced, and starred in a musical he called *The Sound and the Fury,* loosely based on the widely assigned but seldom read William Faulkner novel with that title. Loosely is the operative word.

Just as a nuclear explosion comes from the splitting of a single atom, this full-length musical seems rather to have emerged from Gram Parsons's story song "$1000 Wedding." (For what it's worth, one of the characters named in the song is a certain Reverend Doctor William Grace, but at this point I make no judgment on whether Grace is Gram; read on for my take.) The wedding song originally ran to nine minutes; the three-minute recorded version crops out so much it leaves the listener with nothing but questions. As if overcompensating for that swerve, Grace's own opus swallows and partly digests one novel, a couple myths, some personal histories, and evidently a bad trip or two.

The play, like Faulkner's novel, is divided into four sections—one each in the voices of Quentin, Jason, Benjy, and Dilsey—but Grace added and deleted characters and plot lines with reckless disregard, prompting some to ask if he had even read all of the original text, let alone understood it. Its songs are firmly rooted in country music but it is a music drained of twang and harmony.

Nobody thought it wise to mount the extravaganza in a disused southern Georgia movie house, but those who experienced the production in its original venue would later claim a status akin to that of someone who had witnessed a Babe Ruth homer or a Sarah Bernhardt soliloquy.

The musical dismayed Faulkner scholars, and the few reviews it garnered ranged from terse exposition to outright outrage. The critic from the *Florida Times-Union* called it "kitschy pastiche Brecht." Nevertheless, audiences flocked to the show, and by the third week of production, tickets were almost impossible to obtain.

Two months into its sold-out run, Grace persuaded the Waycross Chamber of Commerce to build a fifteen-hundred-seat amphitheater expressly for his production, and by the time it was completed, many locals said the plans sold their favorite son short.

Faulkner's estate sued, demanding that the production be renamed. The lawyers argued that rather than encouraging a new generation of readers, the play diverged so far from the author's text that it would cause permanent damage to his legacy. The parties settled out of court, and the name stayed (almost) intact.

The soundtrack album, featuring the number one hit "She Smelled Like Trees," turned *Sound n Fury* from a local into a national phenomenon, prompting a backlash from coastal cognoscenti who ranked Grace on a level below even Andrew Lloyd Webber. The backlash to the backlash sent hundreds of thousands of curious pilgrims to southern Georgia, including Elvis and Priscilla and Bob and Rita Marley on an unlikely double date. Elvis subsequently incorporated "White Folks Don't Have Funerals" into his Las Vegas set.

Time magazine put Grace on their cover, acceding to his demand to be photographed in the company of his biker friends at a bar called Skull Ranch. "Masterpiece or Bastardization?" the cover blared; the story inside strongly insinuated the latter.

Georgia governor and presidential hopeful Jimmy Carter attended *Sound n Fury* with his wife Rosalyn. The humble roots and unlikely popularity of the show resonated with his own vision for America, and on the campaign trail the candidate frequently cited lyrics from its songs, always crediting his fellow Georgian and Christian.

Grace himself variously played all four lead roles and periodically added new scenes that probed family and cultural histories barely hinted at by Faulkner. He commissioned fantastic but risky pyrotechnics while refusing multiple offers for touring and Broadway productions. He briefly engaged Michael Cimino to direct a lavish cinematic adaptation until the two had a falling out over the casting of Dilsey.

Late-night talk shows implored Grace to visit; when he finally accepted an invitation from Dick Cavett, he called Faulkner a hack and performed a wobbly version of the Louvin Brothers' "The Christian Life" rather than "Damn That Honeysuckle" or any of the other hit songs from the musical. He married and divorced three consecutive co-stars, moving them in turn into a once grand but now decrepit mansion.

Over three years, eight performances a week took their toll on the creator-director-star, and the inevitable trio of pills, paparazzi, and paranoia manifested themselves. As Grace himself put it, his sins had sins growing on their backs.

✖

Let's pause here and listen a little closer to "$1000 Wedding," the Parsons song some say—okay, your correspondent says—gave rise to *Sound n Fury*, even though it doesn't appear in the musical. Like Parsons, Quentin Compson, the second narrator in Faulkner's novel, was a southern boy who briefly attended

Harvard University. Neither of them lasted very long. Quentin drowned himself just after completing his first academic year; Parsons dropped out after five months to take his band to New York and kick off a successful if erratic career as a rock musician. Quentin is the heir to a once-grand Southern family. Parsons was the heir to the Snively Groves juice empire (his father committed suicide when Gram was twelve).

Parsons's song tells of a wedding that never takes place. The invitations are mailed, the guests show up, and so does the groom. Then a scandalous event of an undisclosed nature takes place. We're given frustratingly little information about it. "I hate to tell you how he acted when the news arrived," the song goes, omitting the substance of the news and saying only that next "he took some friends out drinking," which, depending on the news, doesn't sound like a very extreme response to me. But the gossipy, judgmental voice telling this part of the story lacks the generosity either to spell out the events or to let the poor abandoned (or widowed?) groom off the hook. All we're told is that the canceled wedding cost someone a thousand bucks.

In Faulkner's novel, Quentin Compson's suicide is precipitated by his tattered family legacy and the young man's "deliberate and almost perverted anticipation of death," as well as the marriage of his beloved sister Caddy. The character's bewildered and circuitous internal monologue keeps coming back to a confession of incest that, according to the author, never took place. Quentin's roommate Shreve sees him on the fateful day, two months after Caddy married a man unworthy of her, and wonders why he's all dressed up. "Is it a wedding or a wake?" he asks.

At the end of "$1000 Wedding," the Reverend Dr. William Grace delivers a highly poetic (or mock poetic?) sermon conflating the two ceremonies cited in the song, a wedding and a funeral, without shedding much light on the regrettable events that transpired on this "bad, bad day." It's not clear whether Grace is eulogizing the bride, the groom, or a child that may or may not have come from their union.

✖

As a self-confessed member of the coastal elite, I never saw *Sound n Fury* live, but in researching this story I obtained some grainy but nearly complete footage of a December 1975 performance, and I can confidently say that while it doesn't have much to do with *The Sound and the Fury,* it definitely *feels* Faulknerian. Grace has clearly immersed himself in the life, letters, and literature of America's second greatest novelist (I'll get to the first greatest shortly, but, no, it's not Hemingway). Consider the pivotal fiery scene in *Sound n Fury* (given here in my admittedly imperfect transcription), the scene that on that fateful evening resulted in a deadly real-life conflagration:

> [*The curtain rises, revealing an opulent sitting room with a large stone hearth in which a fire burns at full blast. A gaunt figure in elegant nineteenth-century clothes, his back to the audience, inclines toward the flames. A young woman with curly blonde locks sits on a settee, her hands folded.*]

MAGNUS DEVRIES

Our horses sped us across vast plains
Burning sun, whipsaw wind, the horizontal rain
We tamed the beasts, we tamed the land
We taught the naked savage to be a man
The favor of God I never once doubted
Destiny beckoned for all who allowed it

HYDRANGEA DUPREE

Did you hear their songs and see their art?
Did you feel the warmth inside their hearts?
Do they put their babies to sleep with lullabies?
Do they hold them close each time they cry?

DEVRIES

Such inquisitiveness from one so young
Of all your questions, let me answer just one
The blood in their hearts, unmistakably warm
These worthy adversaries, of admirable form
Some of my men took liberties
They took wives and scalps and victories

HYDRANGEA

But not you, my lord, my fiancé
You would never act that way
I know that you behaved with honor
And most nobly exercised your power

DEVRIES

Of course, my dear, you need not fear
I never took scalps, I took only ears

[*DeVries empties a burlap sack of severed ears onto the
table and flings them one by one across the room. The ears
stick to the walls, then burst into flames, which grow higher and converge amidst a thunderous drone. The walls of
the mansion burn away, revealing a giant flame woman.*]

THE SUN'S DAUGHTER

The liberation is finally at hand
Burning clear across the ancient land
Gods of old I call upon your might
Release the winds, unleash the light
Our day of vengeance has arrived.
Buffalo stampede, snakes uncoil, eagles dive

[*The wordless voices of zoomorphic figures shake the walls*]

Do you hear the Faulkner in that scene? I sure do.

✖

While no recordings of it exist, many early performances of
Sound n Fury apparently featured a solo instrumental inter-
lude on slide guitar during the intermission. The curtains
were drawn, concealing the performer, but knowledgeable
witnesses all agree that the degree of virtuosity exceeded
Grace's (or Parsons's) not inconsiderable musicianship. There
is already mystery enough in this account, but if I were to
plumb the second mystery concealed within the first, I might
call attention to the questionable circumstances surrounding
the premature death of another Georgia icon. Duane Allman
died in a motorcycle crash two years before Parsons's fiery
demise. The two knew each other before either made the
big time, and both appear on Delaney and Bonnie's album
Motel Shot. Perhaps the guitar slinger of the Allman Brothers
(Jimmy Carter's favorite band) and Derek and the Dominos
had fabricated his own demise to escape the burdens of fame,
and it was in fact the Great Oz of white blues shredding behind the curtain. My space here is limited, however, as is my
editor's patience, and so I'll leave this tantalizing path untaken,
a phantom intermezzo concerning a phantom intermezzo.

✖

In October 1976, a fault in the pyrotechnic display during
the Magnus DeVries scene quoted earlier caused the wooden
ceiling beams of the theater to ignite. Eight people were
killed in the ensuing collapse, among them seven-year-old
Veronica Hughes, who hung on for nine days in pediatric
intensive care—a saga reported in ghoulish detail—before
succumbing.

Lawsuits swiftly ravaged the fortunes and good will ac-
cumulated over more than four hundred performances, especially since the producers had neglected to take out adequate
insurance. A penniless and increasingly debilitated William
Grace rejected any thought of reviving his masterpiece. Some
things, he proclaimed, are destined to end in fire.

Having so closely associated itself with *Sound n Fury*, the Carter for President campaign could not avoid being tainted by Veronica Hughes's tragic death. Coming as it did so close to Election Day, this October Surprise may have kept enough Carter supporters home or motivated just enough undecided voters to pull the lever for Gerald Ford.

✖

The cassette Grace had handed me in the diner contained three songs I'd never heard before; they were not included on the soundtrack album, nor were they performed in the footage of *Sound n Fury* that I'd seen. "Mama's Crying" is pretty much what you'd expect, given its title. The second is a rambling *sprechgesang* with an incongruous gospel chorus, called either "Fiddlesticks" or "What Would Your Mother Say?" The standout track is the hummable and heartbreaking "When They Touched Me I Died," which leaves country-western behind for a new, raw frontier. I hope it eventually gets released in some form—maybe Parsons's old flame Emmylou Harris could do it justice.

✖

Does it matter anymore, after all this time, what brought down the Carter campaign? It most certainly does, and not just because, like many others, I believe he would have made a fine president. His vision of America, encapsulated in the acceptance speech he delivered at the Democratic National Convention on July 15, 1976 (I was there in Madison Square Garden), has faded like a dream: "Our party was built out of the sweatshops of the old Lower East Side, the dark mills of New Hampshire, the blazing hearths of Illinois, the coal mines of Pennsylvania, the hard-scrabble farms of the southern coastal plains, and the unlimited frontiers of America."

Sound n Fury is the ultimate proof that America runs on *music.* From "Yankee Doodle Dandy" to Hendrix's version of the Star-Spangled Banner, we are a nation of music fans. Consider the words of Andrew Fletcher, written in 1704, before the United States was even a country, which somehow presage the phenomenon I'm suggesting. "If a man were permitted to make all the ballads," he wrote in *An Account of a Conversation concerning a Right Regulation of Government for the Good of Mankind,* "he need not care who should make the laws of a nation."

It's a more persuasive line than Percy Bysshe Shelley's claim that poets are the "unacknowledged legislators of the world." Poetry is great, but you can't dance to it.

In other words, a fire didn't kill little Veronica Hughes. A ballad did.

And what about the man behind the music? Are William Grace and Gram Parsons the same man? My answer to that question is a resounding *no,* but not in the way you might think. Remember how I called Faulkner our second greatest novelist? To me, number one will always be F. Scott Fitzgerald, who wrote these words in "The Crack-Up": "A man does not recover from such jolts—he becomes a different person and, eventually, the new person finds new things to care about."

Whatever jolts befell Gram Parsons in Joshua Tree, they were literally life-changing, and afterwards he wasn't Gram Parsons anymore. He had become a different person. My fellow Americans, I submit that person's name was William Grace.

THE TUBA TAPE

"To be back! To be back again after all that!"
—D. H. Lawrence

THE TUBA TAPE

Hum subsided into hush as the desert absorbed what was left of a weak, unmotivated storm. Cold air streamed from an open window and a redundant air conditioner in the back of the tour bus. Each bead of condensation on the windows held a pinprick of moonlight. Without shirt or shoes, the slim figure lay completely still, the tattoos on his chest, arms, neck, and face glistening like butterfly wings. His chest neither rose nor fell. The cold from the window invaded the still body in the gloom.

The others on the bus had passed out or fallen into a deep sleep. Bottles of liquor and pills lay everywhere, along with fast food wrappers, track jackets, and a bunched-up wedding gown that had been used to soak up spilled cough syrup.

If he could get up and if they could see him, they would call him by a sound—a baby chick sound, or an Easter marshmallow treat—but that name wasn't what he called himself. He called himself Gus.

If he could get up and if they could see him, they would ask him for something. Money, probably. He had so much of it, fistfuls, Hefty bags of it, and they needed it, most of them being cut off from their families and unwilling or unable to earn a living.

That was the expression. Earn a living.

Gus knew he was dead. That contradictory knowledge fluttered over his lifeless body as the barometric pressure rose and the sky slightly brightened to the east. He came to realize that soon he would be able to get up. He wasn't alive, yet. If a paramedic arrived right now, a world-famous—to some—pop star would be declared dead. The determination would be accurate, but soon, he knew now, he would rise again. His death was an ordeal he had to pass through.

Then he grew more certain he was alive, because he felt cravings. Something salty and a hit of bud would scratch the itch. Where do cravings come from? A loss in childhood, an ancient injury that needs to be salved? Or are they a chemical reaction in the cerebellum or the gut, produced by a colony of sodium-hungry bacteria?

He felt a tune coming on. As long as he was composing—a word he had never previously applied to what he did—he would not decompose.

What is the source of the music that comes out of a person? Is there something called the soul? A function, if not an organ. And if so, has it survived death, too? Have body and soul reunited? Or does the music arise from electrical impulses generated by a trillion interdependent organisms?

A warm spot blossomed in the back of his throat like an oil spill in the Gulf. The toes of one foot flexed involuntarily. He realized he had a splitting headache, a paradoxically welcome sensation just because it was a sensation. Nothing could activate the pain receptors of a corpse. That's not what he was now, or not for much longer anyway.

There was something familiar about the tune, but that's what it always felt like when he came up with something that needed to stick around. It felt like remembering. Sometimes, when he followed a tune's winding path, he bumped up

against a song that already did exist, on someone else's recording—a country hit from the Seventies, or a sample that
cropped up on the remix of a CD-only bonus hip-hop track.
Other times it was a truly original quote unquote work of
art. That's what he hoped this was. Something worth coming
back to life for.

He would get up presently, bear the pain, and drag himself off the bus without disturbing any of his crew. He saw
himself rise and stumble forward, over the sticky wedding
dress. He observed his progress through the bus, but it was
still only happening in his mind's eye. His body wasn't moving quite yet, but his nerves were abuzz, and the stirrings of
an erection moved his loins.

Suddenly, of its own accord, his hand gripped the back
of a seat. With a great effort, he pulled—but did not rise. He
waited some more, feeling the strength gather in his numb
limbs.

The song was taking shape deep inside his belly, its cells
multiplying and generating more heat, which stimulated his
wasting muscles. Nobody woke as Gus struggled to his feet
and, overcoming atrophy and agony, hobbled toward the door.

The tour bus was parked alone in the center of a vast
parking lot. At one end was a strip mall. At the other, a middle school named for an annihilated people. Gus tripped and
fell hard out of the bus, but soon he rose again and headed
in the direction of the school, tracing a wobbly arc as though
drawn by the glow of a sign listing the date of the next PTA
meeting and congratulating the gym teacher on her baby.

He tried the double doors and found them bolted shut,
so he stepped away to look for an open window. Tilting his
head back almost caused him to lose his balance. He dug into
a pocket of his G-Star Raw jeans for his phone, but he fum-
bled it and it fell to the pavement with a crack. The screen
was shattered and unresponsive. Gus cursed and flung it into
the darkness, end over end.

An unwrapped lozenge had been stuck to the inside of his jeans pocket, which (together with his palsied fingers) might explain why he'd lost his grip on the phone. The citrus-sweet sensation churned up a dry spasm in his diaphragm, and he had to shut his eyes to concentrate on holding back the nausea, so at first he didn't notice the ample figure pushing the doors open to see who was there.

"YOU COOL?" The voice was a full octave higher than the man's silhouette suggested.

"Yo," said the superstar.

"WHAT DO YOU NEED?"

"This a school?"

"MM HMM."

"Got a music room?"

"MM HMM."

"Could I maybe just…?"

"COME ON," said the man in the doorway, as though this were a regular occurrence.

They walked in silence past rows of orange lockers and hand-lettered banners promoting kindness and trying hard.

The music room was orderly and well stocked. There were electric keyboards of various vintages as well as every kind of percussion instrument. Orange wall-to-wall carpet shimmered under fluorescent light. A silver sousaphone leaned against a folding chair in the middle of the room.

"You got an 808?" Gus asked.

"IT'S LOCKED UP."

"You got the key?"

"MIGHT."

While he waited, Gus dragged a Yamaha PSR keyboard over to a large gong, found a bench for it, and unwound the cord to plug it in. He rubbed his hands together and flipped the lozenge around with his tongue, trying to moisten his whole mouth. Then he realized that without his phone he didn't have anything to record with. But he remembered he was in a music room, and located a reel-to-reel unit under a vinyl cover, with some sealed canisters of TDK tape.

His host returned with the key and pulled out of a cupboard the Roland TR-808, duct-taped and worn but still operational. On a small table beside it he placed a merveilleux cake encircled by water crackers spread with Roquefort and drizzled with quince jelly.

Gus bowed deeply and started to adjust the settings, his fingers tweaking its knobs with unconscious alacrity. More "Decay." Less "Snappy." He programmed a sludgy four-four rhythm with a shattered glass accent and reached for the play and record buttons on the reel-to-reel.

"YOU GONNA SPIT?"

"You know it," he smiled. He wasn't Gus now, he was Peep.

"THEN YOU GONNA WANT A MIC, I GUESS."

"Shit, that's right. I usually just use my phone, but—"

"I SAW."

"So do you . . ."

"BE RIGHT BACK."

He may have been Peep now, but he was still weary and discombobulated from his overdose and its aftermath. While he waited for the mic, he lay down and let the fibers of the rug tickle his abraded face. The new song blared silently in his brain. He had one last statement to make. He crushed the lozenge in his jaws.

He found himself standing, or leaning, in front of the mic. Someone—maybe Peep himself, though he didn't remember—had programmed the Yamaha to play a vaguely hard-bop cluster to cushion the 808's stomp.

Sorry 'bout your wedding dress
Sorry 'bout this sticky mess
I didn't mean to die like this, Ma
Could I take another lucky guess, Ma?

Could I try again to fuck it up?
If I die again that's twice the luck

He repeated the lines, emphasizing different syllables, and strung together a few more like it, apologizing to his mother but meaning not just her. Readying another verse, he listened to the beats and heard among them a live, organic melody he hadn't programmed. Whirling around he saw his host seated, surrounded by the silver sousaphone. Instrument and player had become one, a splendid creature with a heavenly tone. (Back in the mists of time, this man had achieved fleeting fame on the trumpet, but now he was sensitive about his weight and believed the larger instrument made him look smaller.)

Cool the guy that let me in here
Cool you'll hold it till the New Year
I knew you were a cool guy
Not like them other school guys
Now I gotta get back right
Gotta make the damn track right

He switched off the mic, the Yamaha, and the 808, while his host continued to play as Gus left the room. He trudged across the parking lot, picked up his ruined phone with Roquefort-slick fingers, and climbed back onto the bus. Everyone inside was still sleeping peacefully. He made his way between the seats, back to where he had found himself earlier, and collapsed. Hum subsided back into hush.

✖

What became known as *The Tuba Tape* came out on Soundcloud just after New Year's 2018, under a new account that had uploaded no other tracks. Nobody doubts that it's Peep, despite the absence of any accompanying information regarding where and when it was recorded.

From the Desk of Dr. Eugene Landy

BIGHORN '76

[*4 Oct. 1970*] Patient IX presented with severe depression, which he attributed to recent physical trauma. A rock star famous for his virtuosity on electric guitar, he had lost the use of both hands due to the misapplication of an experimental overdose treatment. (The official story is that IX died of his OD; only a handful of family members know of his whereabouts.)

IX repeatedly insisted that he would have rather died than survive with paralyzed hands. "Why couldn't it have been my legs? Or my ding-a-ling?"

"Your what?"

"I guess you don't remember Dave Bartholomew . . . I would gladly trade my ding-a-ling away forever to get my hands back."

I moved IX into my quarters to allow for round-the-clock clinical sessions, excerpts of which are transcribed below.

—Can you give me my hands back or not?

—I'm not that kind of doctor, but I might be able to help you achieve something even greater.

—Like what?

—Have you ever seen *The Wizard of Oz*?

—No way, man. I need my hands. Hands! Not a heart or brain or courage, and I sure as shit don't want to go home. Plus, the wizard was full of shit, and I'm pretty sure you are too.

—The Great Oz told the truth. Like Jesus, like the Buddha. Are you ready for the truth, IX? Your gift is in your soul, not in your hands. Hands don't write poetry. Hands don't chisel marble. Hands don't prepare a meal or solve an equation.

—Sure they do.

—Do you think we'd be sitting here if your hands functioned but you'd lost your mind?

—*That's* the truth you're hitting me with, Great Oz?

—No, the truth is that your hands were holding you back. The only way to fulfill your genius is to lose them.

—I just want to sleep.

—Lucky for you, I am that kind of doctor.

[*6 Oct. 1970*] Patient IX persisted in his despondency during our second and third sessions, obsessively reiterating his death wish and begging me to kill him. He persevered on the disappointment of fans, friends, and fellow musicians at the idea of him never playing another note on the guitar.

—They'll get along without you just fine. They have Clapton, Santana, Pete Townshend . . .

—All those guys just copy me. What are they going to play now I'm useless as a tree stump?

—Are your roots still growing?

—Huh?

—Beneath the surface, are you still creating? Are songs coming to you that your hands long to play?

—I can't even think about music.

—Maybe that's the real problem, your refusal to think.

—The music isn't in my mind. It lives in my hands. Or did.

—Who are you waiting for?

—Huh?

—You're waiting for someone to fix this. You're waiting for God in the form of a surgeon or healer.

—Isn't that what *you* are, *Doctor* Eugene?

—My degrees are in psychology, not medicine, but that has no bearing on our relationship.

—Our *what*?

—I have rejected everything they tried to teach me in school. It wasn't science. It wasn't medicine. It was a collective delusion broken down into fifty-minute segments. Nobody ever got better. You know why?

—Fifty minutes wasn't enough.

—True enough, but that's not the reason. The sad and glorious fact of the matter is that nobody ever gets better. Healing is the wrong paradigm. Flesh wounds heal, but the soul doesn't go backwards. It changes and strengthens with time.

—I don't have time.

  —What, you've got a hot date? A meeting? A gig? The world thinks you're dead, remember? Outside this room there are maybe three people who know otherwise, and they're not expecting you anytime soon. They have left you in my care. We're alone in the desert together. We have no radio, no TV, no books or magazines.

—What about Carmelita?

—You can trust her. She is here for you one hundred and one percent. Carmelita lives to serve. I believe she is a true saint.

—She doesn't say much.

—She's mute, but her hearing is fine. Her English is good. Carmelita understands everything.

—Does she know who I am?

—The question is, do *you*?

—Back with the bullshit.

—The guitar god is dead. Who are you now? The fans don't want you alive. An imperfect god hurts like a poke in the eye.

—Does she play anything?

—Does she what?

—Carmelita, does she play an instrument?

[*9 Oct. 1970*] Slight changes observed in IX's demeanor. He has less to share in our sessions (no dialogue worth recording), but his mood seems to have improved. He asks about current events. The Vietnam War interests him less than the American Indian Movement's occupation of Alcatraz. He fully supports the goals of the movement and approvingly quotes its spokesman, reminding me repeatedly that he is one-quarter Cherokee. I have left a copy of Dee Brown's recent bestseller *Bury My Heart at Wounded Knee* for IX to "stumble upon" in the small library here. He's also been seen socially in the company of Carmelita, a development I consider welcome.

[*1 Nov. 1970*] I admit that when I told IX he had more to say without his hands, my own expectations for a sequel were quite modest. Now, however, I firmly believe that what he has left to say was not meant to be expressed with a guitar. He needed to lose it, to sacrifice it. That's the meaning (previously unrevealed to anyone, including him) that lay behind his theatrics. Smashing the instrument, shoving it against the amplifier, dousing it with lighter fluid and setting it ablaze. Every time he destroyed a guitar they put another one in his hands. The only way to stop the cycle was to destroy his hands.

[*5 Nov. 1970*] IX is markedly, almost disturbingly, upbeat. He has gotten Carmelita to make him a cape of buffalo skin, with buffalo bone fasteners. He wears beaded moccasins on his feet and feathers in his hair. He speaks in rapid, run-on sentences about a musical ("more than music") extravaganza he's planning, which he envisions as a collaboration between him and another guitarist of American Indian origin named Link Wray.

He showed me a notebook filled with Carmelita's neat, small handwriting in dark pencil. The idiosyncratic musical notation calls for a harpsichord, a theremin, a dozen timpani, a 200-strong reed and string section, and an equal number of children's voices.

This new work, this opera (or whatever it is), this terrible beauty, apparently realizes IX's destiny and may yet give rise to something more terrible and more unstoppable concerning the whole human race.

—It all makes sense now. This is why I lost the use of my hands. Just like Sitting Bull before the first battle of Little Bighorn.
—How did he lose his hands?
—On the eve of the battle, there was a torrential downpour. Fifty followers, including Crazy Horse, entered the sweat lodge and smoked a pipe together before taking turns pledging to fight courageously, then prizing small pieces of flesh from Sitting Bull's arms. He danced and danced as the blood streamed down his sides, until he staggered, prophesied the defeat of Custer, and collapsed to the earth. They helped him on his horse, and he rode into battle, calling out prayers and orders but unable to shoot an arrow.

—Are you some kind of reincarnation?

—My brother Link Wray, creator of the guitar masterpiece "Rumble," *is* Crazy Horse, leader of the Thunder
Nation, and I *am* Sitting Bull. We are preparing for the
second battle of Little Bighorn, a hundred years on.

—Do you know where you are, IX? Do you know who
I am?

—We have to act now to converge on the same spot and
disrupt their blood-soaked Bicentennial celebrations.
Just as the Tribes of Israel returned to Zion, the original tribes of these lands will claim our birthright in the
name of the ancestors whose blood colors the soil.

—It'll be a spectacular concert.

—Not a concert, a battle. People will understand that
when I played the National Anthem at Woodstock it
wasn't an act of patriotism but a desecration of the banner that has given cover to genocide for twenty decades.
Link Wray and I command the power of vibration like
no other musician on the face of the earth. We will shake
the earth's mantle. We will pulverize Mount Rushmore.
We will cause volcanoes to erupt across the plains and
tidal waves to crash down on the white man's cities of
sin.

—I know my history, and if you recall, the first battle of
Little Bighorn took place in June 1876, just days before
the Centennial. The reaction from the nation's capital
in the aftermath of that defeat was swift and decisive.
Indians were massacred in record numbers. There was
no longer any pretense at forging treaties. Grant didn't
hold anything back. You think Nixon will show any
restraint?

—We have something our ancestors lacked. We have the
Black Panthers and the Nation of Islam to join our
struggle.

—You're going to need white faces in your army, too. Lennon, Dylan, Jagger. John Sinclair and the MC5. Abbie Hoffman and the Weather Underground. The Hell's Angels.

—What do I want with a bunch of phony rich honkies?

—For starters, even Nixon wouldn't bomb *them*.

[*Undated postscript*] Shortly after this last conversation, Patient IX left the premises without explanation, and Carmelita stopped coming to work.

From the Desk of Dr. Eugene Landy

THE LUCKY AND THE STRONG

[*11 February 1980*] "Gertrude" is a 36-year-old white female, plain in appearance aside from a Little Orphan Annie wig. She arrived in an agitated state, after a hypnotherapist mutual acquaintance recommended me for my expertise and my interest in popular music. Diagnosis: spasmodic dysphonia—or, as she calls it, kinky throat. Her speech is clear, if rapid, but Gertrude cannot sing. That is, she can't sing in front of people. She reports that usually she can sing when alone, but when an audience is present, she can produce only a painful strangled cough. Whether the condition is psychosomatic is unclear.

—I'm a pretty good singer, too. So when they pity me instead of wanting me, when they look away, that hurts more than the physical pain.
—How long has this been going on?
—You want Gershwin? How about "Summertime"?

—I meant, how long have you had this problem?"

—Who can tell these days? Somewhere between a couple of months and a couple of years. My manager sent me into the desert to breathe the clean, dry air. One of these days I'm going to get my hands on a calendar and figure out how long it's been.

—Did you have addiction issues?

—Booze, pills, smack . . . sometimes in that order, sometimes the other way around. Then I figured out that I could quit anything as soon as I let go of the one thing that lurked behind it all.

—What was that?

—Fame, baby. I couldn't get enough of the adulation. I just had to be loved by millions, which meant I had to send love out by the aircraft carrier. But the world still wasn't getting enough love, so I'd push harder and harder, and that's what started sending my throat into spasms.

—Whereas out here in the desert . . .

—I'm nobody and loving it. Sometimes I can actually even sing again at will. Once in a blue moon.

—Rodgers and Hart.

—I knew I'd like you.

[*12 February 1980*] An unbidden diatribe about Vietnam featuring an impossible-to-follow cavalcade of people she calls personal friends: Henry Kissinger, Jane Goodall, Martin Sheen, Malcolm X, Gloria Steinem. It isn't clear to me that she knows the hostilities have ended. She reserves her greatest scorn for a little-known music critic for the *Village Voice*.

—That son of a bitch. I haven't forgotten what he did.

—What was it? I'm sure you had your fair share of bad reviews.

—This is the verbatim quote: "The U.S. Air Force could save millions by using her jet-plane melisma to strafe Viet Cong holdouts." That was it for me. From then on, every time my voice climbed toward a climax, his words zoomed along and shot my larynx down. I could actually taste the blood.

—Who cares what a rock critic writes?

—He silenced me. He made me realize I belonged to the military-industrial complex as much as Boeing and Lockheed.

—How do you figure?

—Picture a boardroom with five-star generals and captains of industry. What do they want more than anything? Money. How do they get it? Perpetual war. And how do they guarantee that the college students won't derail the gravy train? Distract them with three things: sex, drugs, and rock and roll. In other words, yours truly. I *am* the Vietnam War, baby.

—You sang about peace and love.

—And the merchants of war and hate applauded every moment.

—Vietnam was a tragedy, but your music brought consolation to so many.

—Tell that to the boys from Thomas Jefferson High School, class of 1960, who couldn't join us for our ten-year reunion. Tell it to their parents, their sweethearts. I saw their faces and knew what they were thinking. They blamed it on me, and they were right.

[*14 February 1980*] Gertrude leads a circumscribed existence. Apart from attending our sessions, she rarely goes anywhere in her beat-up VW Beetle except the library, where she has a bantering friendship with the librarian, and the grocery store, where she has a passive feud with the checkout girl.

—You should see the way she looks at my Fish'n'Chips
  TV dinners and mint-chip ice cream. My eyeliner of-
  fends her.

—How can you tell?

—A woman can tell. I wish I could put her in her place
  by telling her I played Woodstock and slept with Joe
  Namath—as if she'd even know who that is. Instead, I
  go back to my stupid trailer—mobile home, I mean—
  preheat the oven, and turn on the TV to catch *As the
  World Turns.*

—You like soap operas?

—Baby, I *am* a soap opera. Adultery, amnesia, hysterical
  pregnancy, split personalities. Just about everything but
  an evil twin.

—Tell me about singing.

—I am the main attraction of my double-wide mobile
  home, but there are neighbors, so I have to keep it
  down. I prance on the couch, swinging my arms over
  my head, belting it out, but sotto voce, along to the
  radio . . . Then, mid-verse, I'll suddenly wonder if I removed the cellophane before putting the Fish'n'Chips
  in the oven.

—Could you sing for me now?

—Here, now? Trust me, I sound amazing in the trailer.
  I'm a stealth bomber now, baby. You should have seen
  me climbing on the roof to extend the antenna. The
  wind nearly blew my wig off. I must have looked like
  that song, "Possum up a 'Simmon Tree."

—Merle Travis. What are some songs you've liked lately?

—Do you know "Killing Me Softly"?

—I might. How does it go again?

—Very funny. Roberta Flack's all over the charts with it.
  You know, Lori Lieberman actually came up with the
  idea after seeing Don McLean live at the Troubador, but
  then these two men, Charles Fox and Norman Gimbel,

came along and took all the credit. I could actually play you a tape of me singing it with a band over at the library.

—So you could sing with other musicians in that room?

— The old hose is usually tangled and kinked, but sometimes all the sudden the flow revives. I get a song in my heart, call up the librarian, and race over there before it kinks up again. The blood beats a rhythm in my veins, and my voice gets its suppleness back. I can't muster more than one or two takes, but usually one is all we need.

—Have there been other songs the hose has unkinked for?

—"Wish You Were Here," by Pink Floyd. The Bee Gees' "How Deep Is Your Love?". Of course, I got to know Barry Gibb after I did "To Love Somebody," though I still don't get the disco thing. Rodney Crowell's "Till I Gain Control Again," which probably comes the closest to "Me and Bobby McGee."

—Those would make a great album.

—The greatest comeback album of all time, baby.

[*4 March 1980*] Gertrude arrived in a notably exuberant mood. A new hit record is (temporarily) releasing her from her disease.

—Bette Midler sings it. She does a good job, but I can do better. There's something about this song that feels just right for me. It's my song. The world just doesn't know it yet.

—I have to ask, Don't you know?

—Don't I know what?

—Is the song called "The Rose"?

—That's the one. Can I lay it on you, doctor?

From the Desk of Dr. Eugene Landy

THE FIRST STONE

[*10 July 1994*] After having my hands full with one para-noid genius named Brian for the past couple of decades, I wasn't particularly thrilled to meet, let alone treat, another. However, a close friend (who also happens to be a powerful friend) prevailed upon me to have a conversation with him. Besides, I have always admired this Brian's style as well as his recordings. When he came to see me in the suite I keep at the Sands, his appearance was notably less spectacular than it had been in his prime, but rhinestones on his chemise and jeans hinted at past glamour.

— Nice place you've got here.
— The Sands is great. This used to be Peter Lawford's suite. Would you like me to get you a room?
— Thanks, but El Morocco is where I belong right now.
— Didn't you spend time in the actual Morocco?

—There's something far more important to me at the motel than anything in North Africa. I'll show you some
time.

—I'm glad you're happy where you are.

—Working on something big.

—A second act?

—How do you mean?

—Well, you founded one of the greatest bands of all time.

—Oh, we're just hitting our stride, trust me.

—They've had a lot of success without you.

—I'm still very much in the band. I'm the leader.

—A lot of people probably think otherwise. That it's
Mick's band now.

—Mick is the singer. Keith is the guitarist. I'm the Holy
Ghost. They're nothing without me.

—You haunt their sound, or something like that?

—It's still *my* band, literally and figuratively. The lips and
tongue logo that they started using shortly after I went
away? C'est moi.

—Looks like Mick's mouth to me.

—Don't be naïve. Kali, the Hindi goddess of death, inspired the design. The logo is my stand-in, watching
over the band all these years. And it's all been leading
up to this moment.

--So this has been in the works a long time.

—Ever since they played Hyde Park on July 5, 1969, two
days after I had supposedly died.

—That was a bit cold, I admit.

—Not at all. Mick left clues so obvious that any idiot
could see what was going on. The poem he recited:
*Peace, peace! he is not dead, he doth not sleep, he hath
awaken'd from the dream of life . . .*

—People should have realized you were still alive.

—He was laying it on a bit thick, I thought. But my wife
always tells me the audience is half morons, half idiots.

[*15 July 1994*] The subject's airtight version of events almost confuses me about the actual sequence of events. I find myself wondering where the band's well-known skill at manipulating the media and controlling their image ends and reality begins.

—Do you ever hear from Mick and Keith?
—All the time, man. Just think about all those songs they dedicated to me. "Waiting on a Friend," "Miss You," "Emotional Rescue." Can you believe they went all the way back to Morocco to record with the Master Musicians of Jajouka? And now they've released an entire album practically begging me to come back in time for the silver anniversary of my supposed demise.
—Do you have to play it backwards to get the message?
—No, man. Every track is an engraved invitation. Wasn't I the one always trying to get the band to use something besides bloody guitars? This album has it all: fiddle, penny whistle, bajo sexto, accordion, trumpet, all manner of percussion. Who did they recruit for guest artists? Two of *my* heroes, Bobby Womack and Bo Diddley. They even named it *Voodoo Lounge.*
—And?
—*Voodoo*, the Haitian science of re-animation.
—And what does Lou Navarro have to do with all of this?
—It was his idea: A rock star dies, but later makes a triumphant return from the dead. He first proposed it to Bob Dylan, who turned him down flat. Then he tried John Lennon. Lou thought Yoko would love it. *It's the ultimate conceptual art project.* But she flipped her wig.
—So you were the first great rock star sacrifice.
—You might say that. Dylan tried to talk me out of it, but he had to admit it had panache. Did you know he paid for my coffin? How many people get to personally thank the man who bought their coffin? Bobby can

keep a secret, I'll say that for him. He still finds a way to visit every few years. The man's always touring.

—What was the original plan for your return?

—I expected the gag to go on for a year. After five years, I started to wonder, but by then my work at the Lib'ary and a succession of new projects were taking up all my time. And now I'm a married man, which changes everything.

[*20 July 1994*] I had feared I was facing an ethical dilemma, since a chief object of Brian's delusions, *Cuckoo's Nest* publisher Lou Navarro, also happens to be the friend who engaged my services. But this disclosure was greeted enthusiastically.

—Are you kidding? This is perfect. You'll have to let him know I'm finally ready. We're going to make history. Not just music history. My wife is going to love this.

—Lou's going to sell a lot of magazines.

—He deserves it. He's been there from the start. The man has always had a hard-on for the band, and for me above all. He used to say the Stones *were* rock music, and I *was* the Stones. At first I would say, *No, Lou, not li'l ol' me,* but he would insist, and that's what led to this routine about God and Jesus and all that. One night in the Waldorf-Astoria, he and I got bloody higher than ever before; one of us would proclaim something serious, and the other would burst out laughing, and vice-versa. Keith and Mick came by, and we let them in on the gag, or the plan, whichever it was.

—That was when?

—It must have been the night before we recorded "Jumpin' Jack Flash." Those three little words from the last hit I played on, they were a magic spell that imbued Mick with the power to speak in my voice. They became my voodoo doll from that moment on.

—The three words were "Jumpin' Jack Flash"?

—No, "I was drowned."

—You talk about Mick and Keith. What about the other guys?

—Bill and Charlie never cottoned on. They were rhythmically skilled, but they had absolutely no imagination. "But we're musicians," they moaned." "Sure," Lou replied, "but these three are *gods.*" I thought he was Saint Peter. The loyal disciple who designed the church. Not the church-as-building but the church-as-business. Christianity had had its run, and it was up to us to organize the new church. We were the deities; and *Cuckoo's Nest* would be the Bible. But it isn't a bible at all.

—What is it?

—A Book of the Dead. You need to read every issue to see the pattern. I have the entire run at the lib'ary. Starting with my "drowning" and the Hell's Angels stabbing a fan at Altamont and continuing for twenty-five years.

—There were some bright moments in all that time, too.

—Not compared to the Manson Family, the Zodiac Killer, the Dating Game Killer, the My Lai Massacre, the Jonestown Massacre—(and don't think I haven't heard of the Brian Jonestown Massacre, not too shabby)—Sid stabbing Nancy, the shooting of John Lennon and Dimebag Darrell. Eleven trampled Who fans, the matricidal drummer of Derek and the Dominos, the irradiated Karen Silkwood, the KKK, the American Nazi Party, and on and on.

—Maybe it's just me, but I still hear a little bit of sex in the music.

—Rock music, according to *Cuckoo's Nest,* provides the soundtrack to a vision of an irretrievably fucked-up America that is always on the eve of destruction. This is no country for laughter, orgasms, dancing, or any kind of celebration. Every party is apocalyptic. Every concert has the makings of tragedy. Every drumbeat is a bludgeon.

—Some people hear it and all they want to do is dance.

—If they do, they're missing the point, which is what my wife is always saying.

—You want me to ask him to send a message to the band?

—Tell them I'm ready. Tell Lou *Cuckoo's Nest* can have the exclusive.

[*26 July 1994*] Brian had been missing since our last session. I reached out to Lou, but his people said he was dealing with urgent personal matters, so I decided to conduct some investigating on my own. The place he calls the Lib'ary was tightly shuttered, so I went over to El Morocco. There was no answer when I knocked on the door of his room, but looking down I saw the corner of a white envelope sticking out from under the door. Inside was a telegram.

```
ACKNOWLEDGE RECEIPT OF REQUEST AND REGRET MUST ONCE
AGAIN DECLINE STOP MAYBE NEXT YEAR MATE STOP MJ
```

A slight vibration in the building's foundation drew me down the stairs from the hotel lobby. It was too rhythmic for an earthquake, and it continued steadily. An unmarked door in the basement led me down another flight of steps, and then another. Luckily, the rack of antique tools at the bottom included a working carbide light.

On the other side of a tarp curtain, I followed the sound along steel rails running through a tunnel that must have been part of an abandoned mine. I became more certain of my direction when the path began to be littered with plastic Baby Alive dolls. Some had their heads bashed in, some had one eye gouged out, others had been defaced with red marker, but they all retained their innocent, hopeful expressions.

The blooming, buzzing noise led me onward. The dolls almost seemed to dance to the pounding rhythm.

Around a bend plastered with posters for appearances by a band called Abortiodontist, the tunnel opened into a glistening cavern, at the center of which an emaciated figure hunched behind a stack of amplifiers. Seated on a wooden stool, she wore a gown of yellowing tulle and a drab cardigan and brandished what appeared to be an electric lute with three necks. Strands of bleached and unkempt hair partly concealed a stubbled face and eye sockets housing a pair of gleaming baby blues that had graced the cover of Cuckoo's Nest more than a few times in the preceding years. Barely intelligible vocalizations dripped onto a microphone from her chapped and lacquered lips.

In that vast subterranean chamber, notes became chords and harmonics became symphonic. Then an even louder crash shook the walls. I turned and saw Brian swinging a massive mallet toward a gong that stood a good three feet taller than him. A devilish grin contorted his still-handsome face.

"Dr. Landy!" he exulted. "Did you bring Mick?"

THE SABBATH BRIDE'S TESTIMONY

When I bring them into the land flowing with milk and honey that I promised on oath to their fathers, and they eat their fill and grow fat and turn to other gods and serve them, spurning Me and breaking My covenant, and the many evils and troubles befall them—then this poem shall confront them as a witness, since it will never be lost from the mouth of their offspring. For I know what plans they are devising even now, before I bring them into the land that I promised on oath.
—Deuteronomy 31:20–21

THE SABBATH BRIDE'S TESTIMONY

Belgrade cried her name.

Wobbling on three-inch heels, she kept her back to the massive crowd that had assembled to watch her fall, to watch her fail. In this entire part of the world, the guys in the band were her only friends, and she searched their eyes for solace as the hungry roar drowned out the amplifiers. Her nostrils filled with the odor of the nearby Banjica concentration camp, active a few short decades ago. The Serbs wanted more than her failure. They wanted her extermination.

The contract had explicitly required her to perform her international hit. By refusing to sing it, she would effectively forfeit three million pounds. Yet her very survival hinged on not performing the hated song even one more time. What had originated as droll self-mockery had metastasized into ritual self-immolation. Five letters, two syllables, and one endless downward spiral. The crowd, even those who "loved" her, craved the song's logical conclusion. The song demanded its own fulfillment. It was the noise her blood made in her brain when she closed her eyes.

The stage tilted one way, then the other. She wanted to approach the microphone stand, if only to tell everyone to go home, but whenever she took a step toward it, it slid away from her.

She needed to pee and vomit.

She wanted Blake. She hated Blake.

It wasn't nausea encroaching; it was death. If she were somehow to escape, she promised herself she would return to the island where she'd last felt peace.

The band played a song she'd written herself and sung a thousand times before, but the first line wouldn't come to her lips. Something about a man and his dick.

The last image in her mind before she blacked out, perhaps suggested by the roar, was the crashing of waves. She surrendered to the indomitable surf.

✼

Serbian police officers and pathologists crowded the intensive care unit, waiting to arrest her in case she woke up, to slice her open if she didn't. She sensed their presence and kept her eyes closed.

She had gone under three times but had somehow survived. She would go back for more of . . . that word she would never say again, let alone sing. She would go back and stay away forever.

She was through with music anyway. What remained for her to accomplish? She had duetted with Tony Bennett and been arranged by Quincy Jones, who had arranged the incomparable Dinah Washington. She'd gone to number one and gone platinum. The career she had dreamed of, fought for, nearly died from, was over. The drugs hadn't finished her off, but the music had.

"See that?"

"Her eyes opened. She's awake. We've got her now."

"Not so fast, mate." One of the men around her bedside turned out to be an agent of the singer's solicitor, an Australian with a thick red mustache and an offhand way of explaining arcane legal matters. Evidently, an obscure nineteenth-century statute of the old Kingdom of Serbia, never repealed, permitted "misadventurous Hebrews" to avoid incarceration if they entrusted their mortal souls to the care of a fellow citizen of royal blood.

"Who's going to take *her* on? Prince Charles?"

"I don't suppose you've ever heard of Melanctha Plant."

✖

From London's point of view, the Caribbean beach might as well have been the surface of the moon. She could walk forever and never arrive anywhere.

The moon moved the sea around, and wave by wave, the sea made the sand. Therefore, the moon made the sand. She would have to remember to tell Melanctha. What pushed the moon through the heavens? The earth's great mass, which both caused and was caused by gravity. Invisible attraction constituted the universe. Here on Earth, it resulted in life, pain, and love songs.

Despite their training and magnificent physical condition, astronauts could not survive long in zero gravity.

Returning to her cabin exhausted and moon-drunk, she realized that not once on her journey had Blake crossed her mind. Or was it like the story of Jesus carrying us in troubled times? Were those footsteps on the beach hers or Blake's? She would ask Melanctha. Melanctha would understand the question.

All the women wore identical gray smocks. Meals and chores set the pace of life on Saint Lucia. The women swam in the sea, walked on the beach, and polished conch shells that would be sold in a gift shop on another island.

Melanctha, who claimed descent from Plantagenet kings on her father's side (as well as a blood relationship to Robert Plant), had inherited the island estate and built a minimalist adobe compound for the practice of her unorthodox theories. Amy had never set eyes on her, but she was reportedly a slight birdlike woman of indeterminate age. It was said that she delivered an hour-long lecture every morning in a gentle but unyielding tone. Amy was not yet permitted to join the assembly in the great room to absorb Melanctha's views on history, evolution, the cosmos, and personal fulfillment. According to two other guests—both blonde, one exquisitely beautiful—attendants wordlessly served them porridge and coconut water. Nor was she invited to the nightly bonfire reserved for Melanctha's seven favorite disciples.

The women weren't allowed to socialize, so information was conveyed in hurried whispers. Also forbidden: makeup, fragrance, sweets, reading, writing, and activity that caused perspiration.

Amy asked if she could sing and was told, *Not yet.*

"The more you resist music, the more it pleases Melanctha."

Well, they couldn't stop the music in her mind. She didn't hum. She didn't tap her foot. She didn't sway her burgeoning hips. Although there was an unmistakable lilt to walking on the beach and an insistent tempo to polishing shells, these rhythms never troubled her body. It wasn't quiet on the island, but it was devoid of melody, something she could never have said about London.

Even though she had never seen, let alone spoken to, the mistress of the compound, Amy adored her. Melanctha's sentiments and prejudices colored every muscle movement, every syllable of her internal monologue. *What would Melanctha say?* was the constant unspoken refrain, hanging in the air like a watchful seagull.

✖

"Melanctha invites you to the bonfire tonight, Ms. Waterhouse." It was the less attractive blonde, standing outside the cabin, her voice tremulous.

Amy liked the new name. What would Blake say to that? Who cared? Maybe he was really out of her life, now that her life was over. She was alive, yes, with a pulse and a warm body, but her life had ended on July 23, 2011. By now it must be November or December at least. She wanted to ask the attendants but felt embarrassed.

The bonfire! Joining the seven elect women around the fire mattered more to her than headlining Glastonbury. Millions had bought her CDs or watched her on YouTube. Some fans were so sweet. They knitted her scarves and wrote her poems. They tattooed her lyrics on their skin. She recalled mascara-darkened rivulets running down their faces, but once her career had outgrown small clubs, the fans ceased being people and became a collective force, like wind or gravity. But the music they devoured so greedily wasn't for any of them. It was for Blake, which is why the fans were never satisfied. Each song made them hungrier and more savage. The word *crowd* made her shudder.

It was a shame that life had to end, but it did have to end. She was lucky to have survived so long. She had made it to her twenty-eighth birthday. The bonfire awaited. She plucked a bunch of crimson flowers, ground the petals between two volcanic rocks, and applied the paste to her cheeks and lips.

Whoever came to the bonfire, she wouldn't be performing *for* them. She would be doing something—she wasn't sure what—*with* them. There would be no crowd, only palm trees and night birds.

Besides the primitive cosmetics, she had disobeyed Melanctha's edicts in two other, minor respects. First, she had accepted candy—hard, sticky polyhedrons wrapped in waxed paper—from the daughter of a fisherman, a deaf child with a dirty face but meticulously braided hair. Unaccustomed to short nails, she spent a ridiculous amount of time scraping the paper off the sweet before sliding it onto her tongue. Second, under her bed she kept a milk crate of tattered Harlequin romances, which she read in the first light of dawn.

Warped by sea air and stained by previous fingers, their pages came easily out of the bindings, but she could fill in the gaps of each story. Doing so made her feel personally, dangerously involved in the storylines. The damsels ran together like grease stains in a puddle, but the heroes enthralled her. Broad shouldered and brooding or debonair and silver-tongued, they whispered to her through the chinks in predictable plots. She could feel their breath on her neck and their calloused hands on her cheek.

Rereading her favorite titles—*Bound by Passion, Nights Forbidden, A Kiss After the Tempest*—she skipped ahead to displays of machismo that quickened her pulse. Fist fights during rescues, cars racing through mountain passes. She imagined the heroes gripping her by the wrist, more roughly than necessary, and leading her off the island, sailing into the sunset. It helped blot Blake out. Any of these brutes could beat him to a pulp, and in her dreams they did.

Nobody had said what would happen at the bonfire. She had no concrete expectations, just a giddy sense of almost mystical possibility. Her world had shrunk from international festivals to these few people, Melanctha and the others, and it fit her in a way that the previous one had not. She would embrace whatever the bonfire offered. She would endure pain, if that was what the bonfire wanted of her. The pain wouldn't hurt all that much, or if it did, it wouldn't last long. The debasement would squeeze tears from her eyes and inflame addictions she'd never quite left behind, but if Melanctha thought it was for the best, she would submit gladly.

Flames would lick the night, burning smells paint the air around naked limbs and tangled locks. There would be nothing left of the trashy pop star trailing tribulation. All that would be burned away to permit new growth.

There were no mirrors on the island, but Amy knew she looked tan, healthy, plump, and wild. She was becoming the Maccabee queen she was born to be.

In the gathering dusk, a twig snapped, sand crunched, and a throat—it seemed—tried to clear itself, but Amy dismissed these sounds as the imaginings of her overexcited mind. She applied another dab of forbidden color to each cheek and left the hut.

Distant leaves reflected the bonfire light, and she had started to pick out a path toward the gathering when they fell upon her, two of them, three times as heavy. She couldn't even gasp, let alone cry out. Her attackers were female, that much was certain, and despite her fear and confusion, this was cause for some relief. It was still a colony of women.

She wondered if this was her swift punishment for the makeup. Other misdemeanors crossed her mind. How would she explain away the paperbacks? What penance could she offer? It was somehow thrilling to have been noticed by Melanctha, to be dragged to face her judgment—if indeed that's what this was.

"We have rules," came a voice she recognized as belonging to the exquisite blonde, a voice as sharp as the fingers that tugged on her armpit. "No exceptions for pop stars."

"You're not the star here," said the other. "There's only one star here."

"Good, bec—" Amy started to answer, but they didn't let her finish.

Was she being taken to—or away from—the bonfire?

She would explain it all to Melanctha. She understood now how to live without music or love. She could stay here on Saint Lucia to forget and be forgotten. She would do the work and follow the rules and let the Caribbean wind erode her features.

If a song or rhyme or chord did happen to pop into her mind, it would boil like a gob of bile in her throat and she would spit it out on the sand. She would let the rhythm of the surf envelop her.

And love. What more was there to say or do? None of the men in the trashy novels she kept under her bed reminded her of Blake. They were chiseled granite, not mottled flesh. They were perfect and bland, invulnerable to the blandishments of song.

Her captors dragged her to a cove and beat her more, continuing to hurl abuse at pop stars.

"With their limousines."

"And magazine covers." The beauty had a bloodthirsty note in her voice, but it was the other one who hissed the decisive word.

"And candy."

Amy broke free of their grip. "What?" Amy's heart revved against the pain that saturated her face and chest.

"We *know*," the beautiful one said.

"The fisherman's daughter told us."

"Told you what?"

"Don't play dumb."

They pummeled her until they grew bored and left. Amy remained in the cove for hours, crying, bleeding, and fitfully sleeping.

✖

Beach gave way to rainforest just as day took over from dawn. The still air hung thick with tropical rot. Amy snapped a branch from a tree as a weapon against snakes and other island threats.

The squall broke like the cracking of a whip. The night sky empurpled, assaulting the island with hailstones. Gales tore palms from the soil. Amy burrowed into the soaking earth, craning her neck for a gasp of air in the intervals between gusts. The storm raged for five or ten minutes then lifted as suddenly as it had come, but she remained fetal in her watery burrow for another twenty at least, letting the dregs of her saliva dissolve the remaining candy barnacled to her molars.

In the morning she would traverse the island in search of a raft or god-knows-what to carry her god-knows-where. She didn't want to die; besides that she had no plan. She scrambled over a volcanic boulder and shimmied up a sticky trunk toward what looked like a mossy plateau to gain a view of her surroundings.

A shaft of lamp light swung above her, and she flattened herself against the moss to avoid being spotted. Staying low, she looked around. What she had taken for moss was actually plastic grass; she was on the perimeter of a vast, newly black-topped lot encircling an edifice of steel and crystal. A number of shiny black SUVs clustered around the entrance, where the first two men she'd seen in months stood guard.

Overlooking the holes and bloodstains in her soaked smock, they permitted her entry and even gave her a towel, albeit one that was gossamer thin and not altogether dry.

✖

Inside the club, cigarette smoke and blinking displays assaulted her senses and scrambled her short-term memory. The glamor and decadence of an expired era endured in this island hideaway, revealed in the tinkle of ice cubes, the unselfconscious cleavage, the obsequiousness of the staff.

Spotting a placard for a Judy Garland tribute act, Amy followed the arrows and took her seat near the front just before the performance commenced. For the first time ever, she declined a cocktail. *Sparkling water, please, with three lime wedges.*

At first she only noticed that she wasn't freezing but didn't know why, then she felt the fur draped over her shoulders, tickling her earlobes. She looked up into the kind, if goofy face of her protector, partly concealed by a curtain of black curls, as it bent over her for a passionate, trembling kiss. A kiss after the tempest. She had passed through the tempest, and now she had the kiss, which tasted of honey, rich island soil, and stormy seas. A blood-flavored kiss. She opened her eyes to see the planter of the kiss climbing, a little creakily, onto the bandstand.

The show began, appropriately, with "Stormy Weather." The Judy impersonator had the look down, and the gesticu- lations, and her range matched the target well enough—but the effect somehow fell between impersonation and expres- sion, like a dick halfway out of its fly. Shrouded in a pocket of gloom, a double bass accompanied the singer so unobtru- sively that the effects it generated might have been coming from the HVAC.

Amused then gradually offended by the graceless Garlandisms center stage, Amy pulled the fur tight around her shoulders. Behind the bass, shrouded in a deeper darkness still, hunched the new love of her life, occasionally glancing up from his instrument to beam a crooked reassuring smile.

After "Embraceable You" and "Fly Me to the Moon," the bow on the bass set the opening notes to "Get Happy" aloft, and Amy found herself accepting the invitation, or was she rising to the challenge? Nobody objected when the be- draggled and beaten stranger approached and wove Barbra Streisand's "Happy Days Are Here Again" half of the duet into Judy's "Get Happy," and a warming jolt passed through the audience.

"Judy" invited "Barbra" to return the next night. She took a few solo encores over the ensuing weeks, delivering chestnuts like "The Way We Were" and "Evergreen," and be- fore long the placard outside the hall read BARBRA! instead of JUDY! There were no hard feelings.

Amy Waterhouse agreed to give two performances a night, six nights a week, developing a swinging rapport with her unobtrusive but reliable—and increasingly inventive—accompanist. His name was Marc, and his gentlemanly, almost courtly manner contrasted sharply with Blake's. It turned out he had escaped an encampment similar to Melanctha's on the other side of the island. His ordeal had led him to embrace his Judaism, and though the lovers were both poorly informed about the faith of their ancestors, they did their best to observe the traditions, lighting candles and muttering garbled approximations of Hebrew prayers they had failed to memorize in childhood.

They kept a stick of envenomed Juicy Fruit gum within the antique mezuzah affixed to the doorframe of their hotel suite. They knew of their faith's injunction against suicide but swore they would quit existence rather than return to work camp.

Amy stayed away from Brooklyn shtick in favor of fidelity to the sturdy tunes selected by the diva early in her career. Paul Simon's "Something So Right" and David Bowie's "Life on Mars?" always brought the house down.

Marc grew more ambitious in tandem with Amy's easy, confident way with the material.

"Have you thought about trying 'Papa Can You Hear Me?'"

"I don't know it."

He hummed a few bars. "It's from *Yentl*, a musical film that Barbra directed."

"Maybe they have it in the library."

Yentl dredged up memories inside her she didn't know existed, and soon she was including its songs in their set. There was more literal and less figurative schmaltz in every tune. Her singing evoked looming pogroms, starving livestock, yellow-gray sidelocks, and medieval superstition, while Marc pared back Michel Legrand's orchestration the way sun bleaches driftwood. The audience devoured it. They had a full house the next night, and twelve times a week from then on, for seven years, with time off each year for Amy to give birth to a child.

A tape of one of the latter performances, recorded directly from the soundboard, somehow made it into the hands of a cantor in Shaker Heights, Ohio, who had been planning to mount a solo version of Isaac Bashevis Singer's tale at the Jewish Community Center. The more he played it, the more the voice reminded him of someone.

THE BLACK ARK VERSION

"When I don't hear music, I feel like something is missing, and when I do hear music, then I really feel something is missing. That's the best I can come up with to describe music."
—Robert Walser

THE BLACK ARK VERSION

I normally start these pitches by describing the recumbent-bike rides through unfamiliar neighborhoods I enjoy on Sundays after an early protein-smoothie supper. Stories rush in at me from both sides of the street. The troubles and hopes of the strangers who live there swirl around me like pollen: the moment their doctor broke the bad news, the betrayals they've never revealed to a spouse, the suspicion that the life to which they feel entitled would surely have materialized if not for that one stupid remark.

But I'll cut to the chase, because all of you already triple qualify: One, you possess the investable capital to make you worth my time. Two, you care about the scourge of drug addiction and believe that a crisis of this magnitude, robbing our best minds of their future—and ours—merits a Manhattan Project-scale solution. Three, you've deduced that I am not who I say I am.

Some people have called me a phony, and they might have a point. Some have called me a quack, and to them I say: Listen to my story first and then decide. Some have said I'm really Kurt Cobain, and to them I say: Close, but you've got the wrong blonde junkie rock casualty. I'm the other one, maybe not quite so high in the pantheon, or maybe just late to the ball.

But if I'm him, and therefore not really dead, you might be wondering why I would admit it. Why go to the trouble of faking my own death—then looking on as my wife, my family, and my dog mourned me, only to confess it now to a gathering of investors?

But even if word leaked out, it would only add to the legend, the brand of Bradley. Elvis died in '77, and people continue to spot him in 7-11 and KFC. Each reported sighting only makes the myth burn brighter. He becomes more immortal, more Christlike, more *Elvis.*

Besides, if you blow my cover, you also blow your chance to cash in.

✖

For a long time, I thought music was my gift. I loved the bounce of ska, the boing of punk, the bump and bling of hip-hop, but it all came to me so easily. I never once suffered for my art. It poured out of me like morning piss, and the fans slurped it up. (God bless the fans!) My only struggles derived from inefficiencies in the market, which unnecessarily delayed my band's inevitable ascent, but these also instigated my deeper interest in what I came to understand was my true calling.

Music is not my gift—competitiveness is. By fourteen, I could reliably attain victory through sheer willpower. Belching contests. Circle jerks. Hot-pepper eating. Triumph after triumph. I could have gone into sports or politics or acting with the same outstanding result.

Competition is the law of all living things. From biology to economy, the competitive spirit separates life into winners and losers. Over the millennia, religion and science have tried in various ways to level the playing field or, as I see it, to give

losers a fighting chance. The printing press helped people
with poor memories. The Ten Commandments told us our
primal urges were wrong. Incidentally, the one that really
gets me is the one against coveting. Do they really think it's
possible to stop ourselves from wanting our neighbor's ass, or
his wife—or his wife's ass? And on and on. Christianity gave
solace to the meek. Antibiotics and vaccines enabled the frail
to survive longer than nature intended, to mate with other
weaklings and spawn more of them. But there will always be
winners and losers, gangsters and haters.

Business leaders are the biggest gangsters of all. We're
history's winners, born to lord it over the undistinguished
masses. We don't "empathize" with "victims." Neither term
befits our brand. Or our species.

✖

Brandishing a laptop and Chanel N° 5, Merit Camino turned
up backstage after a show in San Pedro. She introduced herself as the brand architect for a Fortune 50 health care company and said she had a proposal to make to me, in private.
I shooed everyone out of the room and cleared the table of
pizza, weed, and pornography.

"Can I get you something?" I asked.

"Just green tea, please." She wore a hound's-tooth suit
and sadistic saddle shoes. Her hairstyle was severe, like that
of a woman in a Robert Palmer video. Was that an Eastern
European accent, or just pretentiousness?

"Like . . . tea?" I said, as if I'd never heard of the stuff.

"Never mind." The tendons in her neck tightened. "Do
you want to make a lot of money?"

"Is this a joke? Hell yes."

"Good," she smiled. Not much sugar and spice in this
one. More like rawhide chew toys and blackstrap molasses.
"When I ask my next question, which I assure you is not a
joke, I want you to listen to the whole thing and pause before

responding: Do you want to make a ridiculous amount of money—"

"Yes."

"*And* make the world a better place. Even if it means leaving all *this* behind and—"

"Yes."

"Your wife, your child, your band, your dog—"

"My dog too?"

"I'm afraid so."

"You're not really an architect, are you?"

✖

Accustomed to fans and hangers-on, I failed to appreciate Merit at first. She knew nothing of my music and was unmoved by my charm. My stupid jokes bounced off her like bullets off Superman's chest.

"It's funny," I told her. "You're beautiful, but I'm not the least bit attracted to you."

"It *is* funny," she said. "The feeling is mutual, Bradley. Won't that make it easier to work together?"

It took me a little while to catch on to her proposal, too. This was never just another celebrity endorsement deal. It was a multifaceted partnership. When Jay-Z declared (on Kanye's "Diamonds from Sierra Leone"), "I'm not a businessman, I'm a business, man," he was barely scratching the surface.

The company was more than a sponsor to me, and I was more than a face to them. It was my *substance* they wanted, along with my substance abuse, because I was an Olympic-level addict. My sound and my look, my personality and personal struggles—even my goddamn dog—fit the brand like tattoo on skin.

As Merit predicted, my fictional death by overdose made a legend out of surf slob Bradley Nowell. The album came out two months later and yielded three hit singles. I was the avatar of heroin chic at its global peak. She called it

Cobain-ization and admitted she had tried and failed to land Kurt as their spokesman before his all-too-real death.

The contract was an epic poem, but the short version ran like this: I granted the corporation exclusive license to my name, likeness, and voice, as well as my share of the royalties from Sublime's recordings from the instant of my purported death on May 25, 1996. In return, they undertook to pay my heirs one hundred million over five years, plus 0.075 percent of the Sublime Corporation's after-tax earnings. I became Korey Bain (get it?), Chief Substance Officer, as well as patient number one.

Sublime's music lives on, but Sublime today is no longer a band. We are the full addiction recovery journey: intake, counseling, administration of the treatment in a safe, secure, and private setting; peer network access; individualized lifetime follow-up. We incorporated as a pharmaceutical laboratory, a resort and restaurant chain, and a multilevel marketing company. We filed a historic patent inclusive of pre- and post-administration methodology. Therapy, meditation, fasting, and a twelve-week residency all belong to the prescription.

Merit seemed to relish making me feel stupid. Sometimes I played it up, just to amuse her.

"Tell me again why we're doing this. Why me?"

"You score high with the demographic we covet."

"But you don't like me."

"Not personally, no. But at least I recognize my own antipathy as a marketing blind spot we can't afford."

That tendon in her neck tightened again. Was it a flinch or a flex?

"Are you an addict, too?" I asked.

"I'm an ultramarathoner," she said.

✖

Addiction is bad, but appetite is good. We can't live without the body wanting, and even if we could, such a life would hardly be worthwhile. Cravings for food, sex, and, if we're lucky, beauty make the world go round. You are never more alive than when you desire something so bad you can taste it.

To want is human. To want *more* is American. To want *desire* is Sublime.

Wanting the wrong thing too much is the pathological condition the medical establishment calls addiction. Too many families and communities are in ruins because of it. But Sublime doesn't believe in killing desire, despite what our competitors claim. We believe in managing addiction.

Sublimation, said Freud, drives cultural development: "It is what makes it possible for higher psychical activities, scientific, artistic or ideological, to play such an important part in civilized life." As I glide recumbent through strange neighborhoods, sublimated urges and instincts ricochet off every reflective surface. I didn't name the band with that in mind, but, like Merit says, it all adds up.

Why would I join an industry dedicated to mitigating weakness? It's not that I care about people with measles or high cholesterol. (Okay, I do, a little. Despite my bluster, I'm really quite the teddy bear.) It's the fact that I myself have a weakness, and it's one that commonly afflicts the proficient. We all have our Achilles' heel.

Appetite good, addiction bad. This isn't a flaw in my nature. It's a flaw in nature itself, tipping the balance ever so slightly in the direction of the lazy, the talentless, the slow—giving them a chance, albeit ultimately illusory, to catch up with the three percent of the species most endowed with natural proficiency. If, in eradicating addiction for the proficient, I alleviated it for a bunch of worthless junkies, I could live with that.

✖

I didn't just slap my band name on a package. I sat in on all the legal meetings. I summoned Merit and the laboratory team to report on their progress and quickly established there was something they weren't telling me. Was the molecule ready or not? The more questions I asked, the more evasive they became, until it became clear to me that they were acting not so differently from the way I had treated my record label. Keep reassuring the executives who are counting on your product. Tell them you're close, closer, closest, even though you don't actually know if you have something yet.

Pulling an all-nighter might help, or it might not. Chasing a fistful of Adderall with a fifth of whiskey might be just the thing to open your mind just enough to let in that light beam, or it might land you in the emergency room, immeasurably further from a breakthrough that might never happen. When they ask how it's coming, you repeat that you're close, closer.

Once the molecule *was* ready, I gathered there were still issues. The addict patient's state of mind at the moment of covert administration had to be exactly right, it turned out. For it to work, the subject had to be in a highly agitated state but not conscious of taking the treatment. But fostering the agitated state remained more art than science.

"So Sublime has to take you by surprise?"

"Something like that."

Which is how Korey Bain became the first junkie pop star in history to receive co-author credit in a peer-reviewed pharmaceutical journal.

✖

The executive team took several exploratory trips to proposed sites for the treatment center. Cartagena, Quito, Caracas, and Aruba all prostrated themselves before us. Officials displayed a dismal willingness to despoil several square miles of pristine jungle or to displace a few hundred townspeople. They offered us terms we never dreamed of demanding, including total immunity from criminal and civil prosecution.

Merit was really getting on my nerves by the time our research mission brought us to Jamaica. Everything about her was a tad presumptuous, never more so than when she opined on the subject of addiction, which was kind of my specialty, thank you very much.

While the rest of the team attended a party at the prime minister's residence, the two of us found ourselves alone in a corner of our Kingston hotel lobby. Lipsticked and track-suited, she was expounding her theory that everything in the world fit into one of four categories: the sacred, the profane, the mundane, and the misunderstood.

The lipstick on the lip of her martini glass was giving me ideas.

"Without that fourth labile category," she said, "the other three would remain static; it has always been the misunderstood things that made civilizations go."

"So addicts are misunderstood?" I replied. "Or addiction?"

"I couldn't agree more," she smiled. "The point is, we care."

"What exactly do we care about, besides revenue?"

"Sublime cares about people struggling with addiction in the same way a fabulous restaurant cares about people in need of a decent meal. We exist to satisfy our customers."

"*I'm* Sublime," I said. "You're an employee."

"The moon!" she exclaimed. "Look!"

I turned to the window and acknowledged the view. Whatever. When I turned back, she turned confrontational. "Why are we even here, Korey? Sublime doesn't need a treatment center. First we need a molecule, and then we build the treatment around it."

"I thought you said we had the molecule."

"We're on a pointless junket to keep you amused."

"We're in the Holy Land of Stoners."

"You should pay for this trip," she said. "Not the company."

"I *am* the company."

"You're the face on the box. You're Cap'n Crunch."

"You call yourself an architect," I said. "Can you even draw?"

"Can you even see straight?"

"You're my handler," I spat. "Handle *this,* okay?"

She glanced down and made a nauseated face.

"You're my escort," I said.

"I have an MBA from Harvard."

"Okay, so you're my overeducated escort."

Merit reached up to slap me, and I grabbed her wrist. She pulled me close and planted a sloppy kiss. Her mouth tasted like ocean. I couldn't tell if my tongue was probing hers—or an olive from her drink. The kiss continued until suddenly her jaw clenched and the inside of my mouth went numb.

✖

Something wasn't right, and I felt . . . not a craving but a craving for a craving. Spinning around, I headed out into the neon heat. At the bottom of the front steps of the hotel, I stopped before an ornate fountain, where an onyx owl kept vigilant watch over the freshly quarried marble inlaid with jade zigzags. It was capacious enough that I briefly considered taking a dip before hailing a cab.

A white man with money is an obvious target in this part of the world. I don't believe in victimhood. What I got was coming to me as sure as flies come to shit.

"*Ow yuh duh, mi bredren?*"

"I'm fine, thank you. How are you?"

"*Weh yuh a guh tonight?*"

"Take me . . . away."

Dub slithered out of the taxi's speakers for an unknown period of time, until I felt a tug below my navel and noticed the city's lights streaming past the windows at an alarming speed.

We must have been doing ninety. Bicycles and baby carriages fled before our headlong charge. The cab went up on two wheels as the driver hung a right into a narrow alley. Metal scraped metal, spraying razorblade sparks against the Kingston night. Brakes screeched and horns blared as we accelerated toward a crowded café.

This'll be the day that I die. I swear, those words actually came to my lips as I dug my nails into the cab upholstery.

Clearly, being a rock legend remained my chief occupation even after my official demise. *He blew his mind out in a car.* That's what John sang on "A Day in the Life," reporting Paul's secret death. Was Paul high? Is that why he didn't notice the lights had changed? Dylan nearly died in an amphetamine-fueled motorcycle crash, but he roared back with "All Along the Watchtower." A coked-up Miles Davis totaled his lime-green Lamborghini Miura on the West Side Highway. When the paramedics reached him, the bones of both his legs were protruding through his leather pants. Somehow he survived and reached new musical depths with *Pangaea* and *Agharta.* Kanye, too—he fell asleep at the wheel of his rented Lexus and piled into an oncoming car. "Through the Wire," recorded while his jaw was still wired shut, became his first (ahem) smash hit. It seemed an already dead Bradley Nowell was about to attain McCartney-Dylan-Miles-Kanye status.

Ejected onto wobbly feet at a busy roundabout with no traffic signals, I tried to remember just what I had been craving. Literally *and* existentially, why was I here? Women with cleavage and high boots prowled like sharks, leaning into cars, laughing with teeth bared. Kingston's rhythm was still rejecting my body, and though I tried to capture it with my walk, it continued to elude my grasp. I was dancing to the wrong music and breathing the wrong air. Where did my cab go, anyway?

A voice laced with cannabis and menace called out: "*Yuh play muzik?*"

"Sometimes," I said.

"*Yuh waan fi si di Black Ark?*"

I turned in the direction the voice came from and saw gleams that might have been reflective shades and gold teeth. I'm not quite sure what I replied, either *I'll do anything* (as in, whatever you suggest sounds fine to me) or *I'd do anything* (as in, there's nothing I wouldn't do to see inside Lee "Scratch" Perry's legendary studio, especially since I thought it had gone up in flames twenty years earlier).

He spat. "*Nuh romp wid mi. Nuh guh breaking fi mi heart.*"

"I won't go breaking your heart," I promised. "Take me all the way." Or maybe, again, "Take me away."

The gleam melted into the night, and I was left standing beside a tower of old truck tires. Was that what I had just been conversing with?

A child no older than ten stepped out from behind the tires.

"Where did your friend go?" I asked.

"Friend?" The boy's jittery stare told me he too might vanish.

"Father. Uncle. Grandfather."

The child went on staring. I thought about finding another cab, but the name of our hotel eluded me. Something to do with waves or tide. The place with the owl fountain in the courtyard, just off one of the main squares. He looked into the distance and whistled with thumb and middle finger. Another man sidled up, his face mostly covered by a straw hat, his long dark arms paved with sores. He led me along a dirt path past a series of dilapidated corrugated-iron structures. Chickens and mangy dogs chased each other in the gloom. The apprehension I sensed told me I wasn't high enough. The powder from my pocket had become clumped and discolored. A joint I didn't recall being there was pinched between thumb and forefinger, and I finished it off in three huge huffs, stuffing the roach into my shirt pocket to avoid starting a fire.

✱

Greasy tarps covered the equipment surrounding me. The carpet squelched underfoot. Something had battered and scarred the walls, but soul, or voodoo, or something, kept them from collapsing. Poetry and curses were scribbled everywhere. When I got closer, the words somehow got harder to read. A new old man—not the one who turned out to be truck tires, and not the one with the sores on his arms—awaited me in the shadows, but I lacked the courage to face him. He radiated disappointment.

A Gibson Les Paul in my hands was playing a riff from the song in the cab. It was "Rivers of Babylon" by the Melodians. It was also "How Dry I Am" by Irving Berlin. The lyrics were written on the walls, and though I couldn't decipher them, I was singing one line over and over again: "How can we sing King Alpha's song in a strange land?"

Before Irving Berlin and "Alexander's Ragtime Band," there was Stephen Foster, blackfaced ransacker of an enslaved people's cultural lexicon. Everything I had absorbed as a kid stemmed from that original sin. Bob Dylan, the Rolling Stones, Led Zeppelin. White boys who loved Black music to death.

"*Yuh a shaman or salesman?*"

"Am I what? Uh, both?"

"*Yuh haffi choose, Cap'n Crunch.*"

I tried to reconcile the options, but the reasoning wouldn't escape my lips, probably because they continued to chant the line about King Alpha's song.

The rhythms I had trafficked in throughout my career didn't belong to me. They originated in this reverberant soil, nourished by someone else's ancestral blood. They arose from the hoof beats and wing flaps of species my progenitors had hunted into extinction.

Michael Bolton. Kenny G. The Clash.

"Don' forget Eric Clapton," came the voice from the corner of the studio.

"Him too," I replied, without turning around. "He stole 'I Shot the Sheriff.'"

"Him teef 'Swing Low Sweet Chariot.'"

"Is that King Alpha's song?"

"King Alpha's song is King Alpha's song," he proclaimed. "Keep playing it, Cap'n Grunge."

"You have me confused with somebody else. I get that a lot."

The volume loosened the muscles from my skeleton and detached my brain from my skull. The vibration rolled through me in waves. Was there any difference between the vibration and the molecules that vibrated?

The music I was playing—the music that was playing through me—resembled and re-assembled the extinct sound. Every downstroke peeled back another layer, purging the waltz, the Bo Diddley beat, the boogie-woogie, the four-four, the Dick Dale, allowing the stretched animal skins to vibrate the way they had centuries before on another continent.

All of a sudden I recalled that Sublime had recorded "Rivers of Babylon" in 1992. It had sounded nothing remotely like this.

"You defile the song. Now mi defile you." I felt the old man's fingers pry my jaws apart. His other hand twisted the two front teeth out of my jaw, snapping the roots like celery, first one, then the other.

If I was responsible for these sounds, they weren't a product of my consciousness but of my muscles or my blood. The ancestors—someone's ancestors—were using me as an instrument. They hated me. Or worse, they were indifferent.

The man sat in the corner and urged me to continue playing the same song, hour after hour. If songs used to come out
of me like piss, this was a hemorrhage. The roach in my shirt
pocket burned through my chest. The waters of Babylon
spilled in an uninterrupted flow.

✳

Evidently I was found catatonic and shivering in the owl
fountain late that evening. But the next morning I felt better than I ever had before—at peace, completely free of my
addictions.

✳

No other addiction treatment comes close to our rate of success. Sure, it's costly, but when you add up a lifetime of health
care, law enforcement, and quality-of-life savings, we think
you'll find Sublime a worthy investment.

According to our projections, more than fifty thousand
people will undergo the Sublime experience in the next three
years, and Merit Camino can't kiss them all. Thank you for
joining us for this presentation. Merit is here to answer any
questions you may have.

WHO KNOWS WHERE THE FUNK GOES?

WHO KNOWS WHERE THE FUNK GOES?

If you are receiving this missive, you belong to a very small and exclusive group—the collectors not of merely rare LPs but of ultra-rare *recordings*. We're hardly friends, since we are after all competitors for the same treasures. Nevertheless, I feel I should warn you about a pair of pranksters who are targeting us, in the hopes that you can avoid what happened to me. Their motives (aside from sadistic mischief) are unclear, but their methods are devious.

It started when I received a list of rare disks via a reliable acquaintance.

IAN CURTIS RECITES A BEATRIX POTTER TREASURY
 WITH STRINGS

NICK DRAKE SINGS 'CROCODILE ROCK' AND MORE BY
 ELTON JOHN

FRANKIE LYMON & MINNIE RIPERTON, HONEYMOON IN
 MUNDELEIN!

BABY IT'S KÖLN OUTSIDE: A TEUTONIC CHRISTMAS
 WITH PHIL LYNOTT & MAMA CASS

WHITNEY HOUSTON & KAREN CARPENTER: ONE ON ONE

ELLIOTT SMITH SINGS SILLY SONGS FOR NAUGHTY
    CHILDREN

The legendary, the apocryphal, even the purely hypo-
thetical . . . I collect unheard music. Like all of you, I try to
be discreet about my collection. As a somewhat well-known
figure in the field of financial management, I am prey to the
scorn of Occupy Wall Street types and other assorted cranks
and take appropriate precautions in my dealings, managing
acquisitions through intermediaries. But this pair's communication hinted at something truly special that they could not
divulge in their list, so in this instance I let my guard down
and invited them to the climate-controlled Long Island facility where I keep my extensive library of unofficial recordings, along with specially engineered equipment upon which
to play them.

Two young women—one with fine features but a sallow
complexion, the other distinguished mostly by the shallow-
ness of her remarks—arrived with a calfskin valise and a por-
table CD player.

"I'd rather you left that outside," I said. "Digital equipment compromises the environment I've engineered."

"Oh, it's just a present for my niece," the Shallow One
said. "I promise not to play anything on it."

"But you're so right," the Sallow One offered. "Analog
is far superior."

"It's so much more faithful," I agreed. "In that it repro-
duces not sound but vibration. The air in this room vibrates
just the way it did in the studio at the moment of creation.
Come in, just leave that thing by the shoe rack, and please
remove your shoes."

In stocking feet, they followed me to the listening room,
which is lined with shelves holding hundreds of recordings
in various formats, each one vacuum-sealed and affixed with
a barcode. I pushed play on a reel-to-reel deck, and the room

filled with the sound of the freshly bailed-out Sid Vicious improvising on unplugged electric bass with a Bronx bongo player. We assembled in jet-black armchairs positioned between two obelisk speakers.

"Tell us," said Sallow, "Have you ever fallen for a fake?"

"I've certainly come close. I remember one time in particular. I'd received a package on approval, an acetate. A quite astonishing recording. It started with studio chatter, dominated by a woman's voice coated with tobacco tar, talking too fast and interrupting herself to laugh and cough. The sound of clattering cutlery mixed with those of two or more guitars tuning up. Then, in a half-heartedly accurate Elvis imitation, the woman snarled, 'Let's get real, real gone for a change,' and the guitars wove a sturdy basket for her haggard voice. "I heard he sang a good song, I heard he had a style . . ."

"I knew the song, of course—'Killing Me Softly' had long been an adult contemporary chestnut—but it had never sounded as immediate and unforced as this. I thought I knew the voice, too. The man who sent me the recording claimed it was Janis Joplin."

"But you weren't sure?"

"Janis Joplin died of a heroin overdose in 1970," I said. "Her recording of 'Me and Bobby McGee'—written by Kris Kristofferson, as you no doubt know—was released a few months later. Her gift for interpreting other people's songs was just starting to reveal itself. She died two years before 'Killing Me Softly' was written."

"So it can't have been her. But I imagine there must be Janis Joplin impersonators out there."

"I thought of that, of course. But an impersonator impersonates. This singer was singing a song Janis never sang, in just the way she would have sung it. It felt like more than mere impersonation, like something original.

"You can't argue with death, though. For it to have been Janis, she'd have had to fake her own death and disappear completely, and how likely is that? They found her body in that LA hotel room, after all. So in the end I accepted it couldn't be a genuine Janis Joplin recording, it had to be a fraud, and I turned down the chance to buy it.

"I've regretted that decision every day since, and I still hear her voice singing that song. Somehow it seems more likely, even if it's impossible, that Janis Joplin was still alive to record that song than that it was the work of an impersonator."

"Fascinating," Sallow smiled.

"That list you provided," I said. "There's nothing on it that meets my needs. But you suggested there might be something else . . ."

They exchanged knowing glances. "We recently came into possession of an item that hasn't been offered to any other collectors," she said, reaching into the valise. She removed an unlabeled record sleeve from its protective packaging and proffered it to me. Inside was a pristine platter, which I accepted with latexed hands, wordlessly measuring the width of the grooves and selecting the appropriate stylus.

"This is indeed an honor," I noted before setting the record down on a custom-built appliance of teak, titanium, and tinted glass domes.

"I'm sure you know about Sandy Denny's time in Ohio," Shallow said. Clearly this was her part of a script they had rehearsed.

"After her second fall down the staircase," Sallow added. "April 18, 1978."

"I thought the second fall killed her," I said, playing along but intrigued.

"They found her in a heap at the bottom of the stairs in a friend's London flat. Emergency surgery stopped the internal bleeding, but only time brought down the swelling. Her personality shifted over the course of her convalescence. She had been the quintessential Flower Child, the kind who would reluctantly show men her poetry and coyly let them kiss her cheek before breaking down in tears over the idea of starving babies in Africa."

Shallow broke in: "Even before the fall, she had chafed against that stereotype. What was that line in 'Solo'? Oh yeah: 'I've always kept a unicorn, and I never sing out of tune.'"

"And this recording . . ." I said, giving them the chance to get to the point.

"First she went to New York, to hang out at CBGB, but punk left her cold. She wanted to have fun, whatever that meant, and then she happened to hear "Love Rollercoaster" on the jukebox at an all-night diner.

"She decided she wanted to join the Ohio Players and caught the next Greyhound for the Midwest. She ended up in Dayton, the industrial capital of cash registers and funky music."

"Is that what this is?" I asked, pointing to the acetate.

"She never caught up with the Ohio Players," Sallow said, "but she did meet Roger Troutman, who was about to release his breakthrough hit with Zapp."

"'More Bounce to the Ounce,'" I said.

"What you probably don't know is that Roger recorded Sandy on his talk box," Shallow announced.

"I can't say that I did."

"Hardly anybody heard this," said Sallow. "Then Roger died in 1999, setting off a protracted struggle over the contents of his vault."

"His brother shot him," Shallow exclaimed, quite unnecessarily.

"Sandy was sick of her voice," Sallow summarized, perhaps sensing my impatience. "But she still wanted to sing."

I lowered the stylus, and a not unoriginal funk rhythm played for a few bars before a female voice came in, heavily processed by the talk box. Predictable *good night, moonlight, delight* rhymes unspooled in a deliciously quirky cadence. Transfixed by the question of whether this was indeed folk

goddess Denny's high, pure voice, flattened and distorted by
a novelty device, I didn't notice Shallow stand up, take the
Sid Vicious reel from the player, and begin winding the tape
around my ankles and the legs of my chair. By the time I realized what was happening, she had me bound quite tightly,
and I couldn't bring myself to break the ribbon.

My pleas and imprecations went unheeded.

"What do you want to hear next?" Shallow asked her
accomplice.

"You know what might be good . . ."

"I think I do."

Shallow switched the boombox on, and Madonna's voice
burst forth. I dare you to name a more perfect example of
the infectious ubiquity of everything I hate about pop music
and contemporary society in general. Following the robust
acoustics of the acetate, the harsh, thin, agonizingly digital
sound assaulted my mind. "Live out your fantasy here with
me, just let the music set you free."

They collected their acetate and skipped out the door,
laughing as they went and leaving me alone with the cursed
track on repeat.

I wouldn't wish such an experience on my worst enemy,
hence this letter. Let my shame be your gain!

OPERATION BEATNIK

For the eyes of the world now look into space, to the moon and to the planets beyond, and we have vowed that we shall not see it governed by a hostile flag of conquest, but by a banner of freedom and peace. We have vowed that we shall not see space filled with weapons of mass destruction, but with instruments of knowledge and understanding.

—John F. Kennedy

Just keep watching and you soon will see
The moon is made of gold

—Richard Loris Jones

OPERATION BEATNIK

On the basis of previous encounters, It knew It needed a 'cool' human male for It's purposes, but despite extensive research, It could not quantify the properties of the phenomenon. As far as It could tell, 'consciousness' comprised two layers of cognition, the first applying to all the things humans do unintentionally (breathing, digesting, and more complicated processes attributed to so-called muscle memory) and the second to their intentional actions. In 'cool' humans, the two layers followed identical contours without quite touching.

While It could compose music sophisticated enough to make Mozart sound like a jackhammer, It had nothing analogous to popular song. Lyrics, while superficially translatable, did not compute. When Elvis addressed the "Blue Moon," was he sending it a signal? When Sinatra sang "Fly Me to the Moon," was he actually requesting transport?

It was able to gauge precisely the power wielded by the singer at the microphone, which is why, in the wake of JFK's elimination, It shifted It's attention to pop stars. These special beings controlled millions via radio waves and sexual magnetism. Some formed groups for the purposes of merging their

213

individual powers. This technique exerted nearly unbearable mental stress on adolescents reaching reproductive maturity.

It approached Elvis and Sinatra, but both declined. Elvis said his religion forbade celestial travel, while Sinatra was looking forward to two or three parties that couldn't be rescheduled. And they couldn't be coerced—as powerful as It was, It required a willing participant.

According to It's best calculations, the Idol possessed the thinnest detectable cushion between his two layers of consciousness. A vocalist who had left religious music behind to become a pop star, he displayed elegance in his manner and eloquence in his speech, though he danced clumsily.

Invited to consider joining a mission to protect the moon, the Idol agreed so readily that It thought maybe he hadn't understood the proposal. But he had no religious objections, and, having just released "A Change Is Gonna Come," he felt he had nothing left to prove. He had conquered gospel with the Soul Stirrers. Then he had become a teen heartthrob and a chart-topper without breaking a sweat. More than anything else, he was bored.

The Idol made no inquiries as to It's precise origins and ultimate objectives, nor the spirit in which It planned to meet them. He greeted the whole experience as the makings of a story with which he could later entertain the heavyweight champion of the world and the spiritual leader of the Civil Rights movement. His personal destiny and that of the human race constituted no more than the anecdote's backdrop.

✖

On July 31, 1964, U.S. spacecraft *Ranger 7* crashed on the moon after transmitting 4,308 high-resolution photographs of the lunar surface. Time was running out for It.

It's civilization was far more advanced than Earth's but had never developed photography (or indeed any kind of image-making); the whole concept left It mystified and alarmed. Cameras were known to capture something, not just in their immediate range but over great distances.

—What are pictures?

—You mean movies?

—Cameras make them.

—Oh! Pictures are like records, but instead of hearing them, you see them. We take pictures of mountains we like, or pretty faces, so we can take them out later and remind ourselves what they look like.

—Do pictures have military applications?

—There's something called reconnaissance. We spy on them, they spy on us. Spies hide cameras in their hats. For some reason, women love them.

—Hats?

—No, spies. Women *love* spies.

✱

As far as the Idol understood, It had located a replacement with the same build and similar genetic makeup on Skid Row, groomed and dressed him in the Idol's style, and brought him to the Hacienda Motel a few weeks before Christmas 1964. It had then set in motion a chain of circumstances involving an emotionally unstable prostitute and a motel manager with an itchy trigger finger. The manager had shot the impostor in the chest, and It had finished the job by beating his face beyond recognition. Six days later, the shooting was ruled a justifiable homicide.

Back on the moon base, It administered a series of injections calibrated to the Idol's body and brain chemistry. It made sure he was comfortable and plied with snacks and companionship. It created a moon "pad" on a par with a luxury suite at the Ritz-Carlton Hotel and provided canapés, gin fizzes, and a tall brunette with almond eyes and a midnight-blue Oscar de la Renta one-shoulder moiré bow gown. No attempt was made to conceal the fact that the room and the woman were both chemically induced holograms.

Even as the drugs disaggregated his conscious and unconscious activity, a process that would have induced psychosis in almost anyone else, the Idol maintained a disarming congeniality.

—This is a trip. Is that really the Earth down there?

—Yes. Do you recognize the outline of your continent?

—I've always known there was something up there beyond the sky. I looked around me. I studied science books. I'd watch TV, and I'd say, okay man, what else you got? Malcolm and Cassius—I mean, Muhammad—said I was crazy. I really should have bet them.

—But how would you ever collect?

—Eh?

—On the bet. As far as your friends are concerned, you're dead. Your wife. Your fans. The world. All are mourning you right now.

—I can't believe Frank and Elvis turned this down. Elvis would love it here.

—We need to talk about the moon.

—Sure thing, but can it wait until after dinner? I promised her (and as he pointed, the woman's outfit changed from negligee to tennis outfit) a match this afternoon. Man, I am not going to lose to a hologram!

—Do you understand the reasons why It doesn't want humans on the moon? If you're going to make songs against the idea, you need to understand It's position, don't you?

—I'd rather understand why people want to go, and then I can write against that. The people don't know that It exists. If they did . . .

—Maybe a few do.

—Yeah, but nobody believes them.

—It believes you humans might want to mine precious minerals or metals here. Perhaps the song could affirm that the moon is green cheese. There's nothing here worth digging up.

—That's just a figure of speech nobody believes in. This is all because of the Cold War.

—A war?

—In this case, more a race than a war. We want to get there before the other guy. There's no plan to "dig" for gold or anything else. I'm guessing we'll just stick a flagpole in the dirt, snap a few pictures, and go back home.

—It doesn't want humans to aim their rockets at the moon at all.

—And you think music can help stop that?

—We've observed some spectacular effects with this trial message.

Chemically transmitted sound filled the Idol's ears.

Please Mr. President
            (Uh oh!)
I don't wanna go
            (Please don't shoot me into outer space)
P-P-Please Mr. President
            (Uh oh!)
I don't wanna go
            (Please don't shoot me into outer space)

—That was you? That's not half bad!

—Number 37 on the Top 40 chart. The method was confirmed, but It has determined that more nuanced messages are needed.

—This is a great honor.

—We have great logistical capabilities. We're just not that good at popular music.

—Okay, how about you take care of the logistics, and I influence the Top 40. Ever hear of the Beatles? The Rolling Stones? Those British boys love me, man. They keep asking me how I wrote all my songs. They even want to steal my manager away. They say the only one they liked as much as me was Buddy Holly.

—From our perspective, Buddy Holly represented a problem.

—What do you mean, a problem?

It activated the speaker, and a voice crooned "Moondreams can be a sensation, moondreams may be fascination, love can be our destination . . ."

—You killed Buddy Holly? He was my friend, man. We went on the *Dick Clark Show* together.

—Why do you call us that?

—Eh?

—Why do you call us 'man'?

—That's just how we talk.

—JFK didn't talk that way.

—Black people, I mean. It's something we Black people say.

—Why do you keep saying you're Black? We've never seen a Black human.

—Maybe you're not looking the right way.

—Are you upset? We've never seen you upset.

—You shouldn't have killed Buddy. You shouldn't have killed JFK either. Those were good men.

—Was Buddy Holly a Black man?

—No. Well, a little bit, maybe.

—How about a song saying the moon is poisonous or radioactive?

—The people who want to go, when they hear that, will just want to go more. The challenge becomes more enticing. Besides, how is a singer who's never left America supposed to know about the moon's radioactivity?

—What about saying that going to the moon just isn't cool? If someone cool says it, they'll believe him.

—You're on to something with that. You know what the opposite of an astronaut is?

—A deep-sea diver?

—No, man, it's a beatnik!

—What does a beatnik want?

—Beatniks don't want to do anything. They sit around in cafés and talk about ideas.

—What are those?

—You know, ideas! Freedom. Liberty. Revolution. Sexual liberation. Stuff like that. Beatniks smoke reefer and contemplate the sound of one hand clapping.

—What do beatniks think about the moon?

—They think it's far out, right where it is.

—It likes beatniks.

—You're giving me a great idea. With the right music, everybody's going to become a beatnik. You picked the right guy. Elvis and Frank together couldn't have done what I'm going to do.

—This is a beatnik song, is it not?

The chamber chemically filled with the Kingston Trio's wonderbread harmonies: "C'mon people now, smile on your brother. Hey! Let's get together, try and love one another right now."

Once the Idol stopped laughing and realized what It was getting at, he got down to business, embarking on a series of extrasensory songwriting partnerships with some of the decade's greatest stars. He found the process artistically fulfilling. He hadn't gone into the business for the money; it was for the power. And how much more powerful do you get than by redirecting galactic history? However, the technology for transmitting song ideas took more than a year to develop, and the more explicit the message, the harder it was to transmit. What follows is a partial list of the results, along with the limited details available:

- Donovan, "Sunshine Superman" (1966), The first beatnik-themed song to hit number 1 and the official kickoff of the hippie era. Like many songs on this list, the official song-writer composed it under the influence of drugs, yielding a state of mind receptive to extrasensory influence. The Idol had originally penned the line "Superman and Green Lantern ain't got nothin' on me" for a gospel song that the other Soul Stirrers rejected as blasphemous.

- "Aquarius / Let the Sunshine In" (1966), from the musical *Hair.* The Idol hated all the interpretations of this song, including the Fifth Dimension's March 1969 hit version.

- The Rascals, "Groovin'," (1967). The Idol "wrote" every line of this hymn to doing little or nothing and closely su-pervised its recording.

- Otis Redding, "(Sittin' On) The Dock of the Bay" (1967). No performer was more tuned into the Idol's wavelength than Redding. It was a relatively simple operation to im-plant this paean to indolence.

- The Beatles, "Yellow Submarine" (1966) and "Octopus's Garden" (1969). The idea being that underwater is a much more desirable field of exploration than outer space. McCartney wrote "Yellow Submarine" (aided by Lennon and beatnik par excellence Donovan), but since Ringo sang it, he was targeted for the Idol's wavelength contribu-tion, "As we live a life of ease, everyone of us has all we need." Never very accomplished as a songwriter, Ringo himself proved difficult to influence, failing to recognize inspiration when it hit him over the head. His underwater ode came out only just before the moonshot.

- The Youngbloods, "Get Together" (1967). The Idol helped the band retool the Kingston Trio song for the Age of Aquarius.

- Van Morrison, "Brown Eyed Girl" (1967). The Irish singer wrote the lyrics and main melodic line, but The Idol's *Sha la la's* made this ditty about sex in the grass a hit and sent Morrison's career into orbit.

- Canned Heat, "Poor Moon," (1969). Another late-stage endeavor, this song by the hippie blues outfit suggests humankind should leave the moon alone because it's vulnerable and pitiable. Over a pulsating, not-very-bluesy rhythm, Wilson laments, "Well, you sure look good in the sky at night, and it's sad to say you won't shine so bright, some day."

- David Bowie, "Space Oddity," (1969). A desperate last attempt, released five days before the launch of the *Apollo 11* mission that put Neil Armstrong and Buzz Aldrin on the moon. Inspired by Stanley Kubrick's film adaptation of Arthur C. Clarke's *2001: A Space Odyssey*, Bowie was already predisposed to depicting space as a menace. He had taken an explosive combination of drugs while watching the movie, enhancing his suggestibility. The Idol contributed the couplet "Planet Earth is blue, and there's nothing I can do."

✖

Tension permeated the conversations between It and the Idol after that first moonwalk.

—The defensive strategy failed. It may be time to go on the offensive.

—They didn't do anything, man. They planted their flag and went right back home, just like I told you they would.

—Maybe you're not a very good songwriter after all.

—I'm good. I'm the best. The Earth is crawling with hippies now, thanks to me.

—But the men who came to the moon weren't hippies. They had short hair and didn't take any drugs.

—Not big music fans, I guess. Don't go blowing things up over two guys planting a flag.

—It didn't ask for your advice.

—You know, I think I want to go back home now. This has been fun, but maybe we'd better say goodbye while we're still friends.

—You want to go back.

—Yeah, thanks. Just drop me off somewhere in the greater New York City area.

—You can't go back. You were killed in a California motel.

—That wasn't me. That was an impostor, you said.

—There was no impostor.

The Idol took one last look at the blue orb hanging in space.

Planet Earth is blue, and there's nothing I can do.

✖

Operation Beatnik bought It six years, and while a few more humans did set foot on the moon, lunar exploration slowed to a trickle thereafter and eventually dragged to a halt. They lost interest after shooting a golf ball and collecting a few rocks, and It had ample opportunity to extract every speck of gold and other precious metals.

Moreover, with his final composition, the Idol redefined cool in such a way that It can comprehend—and exploit. Indifference has replaced laziness.

Ultimately, the Idol cared too much. It saw the look on his face when told he couldn't return to Earth. It believes the English word (for which no word exists in It's lexicon) is *crestfallen.*

David Bowie, by contrast, responds to each and every dilemma with equanimity (another word not in It's lexicon, but for the opposite reason). It cannot determine whether this attitude originated in his "Space Oddity" experience. Devoid of racial, national, and gender attachments, David Bowie evinces supreme indifference to pain, war, violence, injustice, exploitation, cruelty . . . and while It detects considerable internal alienation, he suppresses these feelings so thoroughly that he no longer feels them. The phantasmagoria of images streaming through his consciousness fails to manifest in his demeanor. Bowies are preferable to beatniks, and as his influence spreads, humanity will be less and less likely to care about It's next plans.

✖

The indifference intoxicates, as you all shrug your way to oblivion.

Let's dance.

NOTES

The introductory epigraphs are taken from Anne Carson's *red doc>*, Donald Barthelme's *Sam's Bar*, and Lucy Sante's "The Avenger" (in *Maybe the People Would Be the Times*).

LIVE FROM AMELIA'S LOUNGE
I believe I can fly, I believe I can touch the sky — from "I Believe I Can Fly," (Kelly), Universal Music Z Songs (BMI).

LOOK MA NO LIVER
My name is my name is spoken by the character Marlo Stanfield in the TV series *The Wire* (2008, series writers: David Simon, Ed Burns, George Pelecanos, Eric Overmyer, David Mills, Dennis Lehane, and Richard Price); the Robert Irwin quote is included in and provides the title of the book *Seeing Is Forgetting the Name of the Thing One Sees: Over Thirty Years of Conversations With Robert Irwin*, by Lawrence Weschler; It was all a dream — from "Juicy" (Combs/Mtume/Olivier/Wallace), Mtume Music (BMI)/Round Hill Compositions (BMI)/Twelve and Under Music (BMI); Cellophane flowers of yellow and green, towering over your head — from "Lucy in the Sky with Diamonds" (Lennon/McCartney), Sony Music Publishing; Woman is the n——of the world — from "Woman Is the N——of the World" (Lennon/Ono), Ono Music (BMI); I could feel my emptiness as Adam felt his nakedness is adapted from Peter Shaffer's play *Amadeus*; I watched myself becoming extinct is adapted from Peter Shaffer's script for the movie version of *Amadeus;* the dream is over — from "God" (Lennon/Ono), Ono Music (BMI).

FOR ART'S SAKE

The extract from Heloise's letter to Abelard from *The Letters of Abelard and Heloise*, translated by Betty Radice (Penguin, 1976); fibers in a variety of colors protrude out of my skin, like mushrooms after a rainstorm. They cannot be forensically identified as animal, vegetable, or mineral—is from Joni Mitchell's description of Morgellons disease in an interview with Matt Diehl, *LA Times*, April 22, 2010; Marrying a queen might not make me a king, but at least I'd have a shot at being a prince—Marvin Gaye quoted by Sharon Davis in her biography *I Heard It Through the Grapevine* (Mainstream Publishers, 1991); If you don't honor what you said, you lie to God—from "When Did You Stop Loving Me, When Did I Stop Loving You" (Gaye), Jobete Music Co Inc. (ASCAP); Seeing myself as a woman . . . I must bear the guilt and shame for weeks—Marvin Gaye quoted by David Ritz in his biography *Divided Soul: The Life of Marvin Gaye* (Da Capo Press, 1985); Couldn't you just love me like you love cocaine—*from* "Ladies' Man" (Mitchell), Crazy Crow Music (ASCAP).

DISGRACED

She swims to the side, the sun sees her dried—from "Gomper" (Jagger/Richards), Abkco Music Inc (BMI); Freezing red deserts turn to dark, energy here in every part—from "20 000 Light Years from Home" (Jagger/Richards), Abkco Music Inc (BMI).

SNOW, MILK, AND PSALMS

Early on, I saw my suffering as my salvation—Jimmy Scott quoted in *Faith in Time: The Life of Jimmy Scott*, by David Ritz; more pain and prettiness in his voice than any singer anywhere—Ray Charles, cited in David Ritz, "The Triumph of Jimmy Scott (1925-2014)," *Rolling Stone*, June 16, 2014; Jimmy Scott is the only singer who makes me cry—Madonna, cited in Joseph Hooper, "The Ballad of Little Jimmy Scott," *New York Times*, Aug. 27, 2000.

THE SQUARE 65 MIXTAPE

Don't call it a comeback, I been here for years—from "Mama Said Knock You Out," (Clinton/Collins/Jacobs/J. McCants/L. McCants/Morrison/Smith/Stewart/Williams), Bridgeport Music Inc (BMI)/Harlem Music (BMI)/Jimi Mac Music (BMI)/Marley Marl Music Inc. (ASCAP)/Rubber Band Music (BMI)/Universal Music Corporation (ASCAP)/Universal Music Z Songs (BMI); I'm always making a comeback, but nobody ever tells me where I've been—from *Lady Sings the Blues*, by Billie Holiday and William Duffy (1956); the lines Billie Holiday sings (What did I know, what did I know / of love's austere and lonely offices?) are from Robert Hayden's poem "Those Winter Sundays."

WAITING FOR THE SON

The future's uncertain and the end is always near—from "Roadhouse Blues" (Densmore/Krieger/Manzarek/Morrison), Doors Music Co. (ASCAP);

See the sunlight, we ain't stoppin', keep on dancin' till the world ends—from "Till the World Ends" (Gottwald/Kronlund/Martin/Sebert), Kobalt Songs Music Publishing; Hello, I love you, won't you tell me your name?—from "Hello, I Love You" (Densmore/Krieger/Manzarek/Morrison), Doors Music Co. (ASCAP); break on through to the other side—from "Break On Through," (Densmore/Krieger/Manzarek/Morrison), Doors Music Co. (ASCAP); It's better to burn out than to fade away—from "My My Hey Hey Out of the Blue" (Blackburn/Young), Broken Arrow Music Corp (BMI)/Hipgnosis (ASCAP); Until you've gone forever, I'll be holding on for dear life, holding you this way, begging you to stay—from "Any Day Now" (Bacharach/Hilliard), Bourne Co. (ASCAP)/Universal Music Corp. (ASCAP).

THE SOUND N FURY DEMOS

Part of this text first appeared in an essay in *Perfect Sound Forever* in 2001. I hate to tell you how he acted when the news arrived . . . he took some friends out drinking—from "$1000 Wedding" (Parsons), BMG Platinum Songs US (BMI); deliberate and almost perverted anticipation of death and Is it a wedding or a wake?—from *The Sound and the Fury* by William Faulkner; bad, bad day—from "$1000 Wedding" (Parsons), BMG Platinum Songs US (BMI); extract from Jimmy Carter's speech to the 1976 Democratic National Convention cited from *The Presidential Campaign, 1976: Jimmy Carter* (US Govt. Printing Office, 1978); A man does not recover . . . new things to care about—from "The Crack-Up" by F. Scott Fitzgerald (*Esquire*, Feb. 1936).

THE TUBA TAPE

Epigraph from D. H. Lawrence, "The Man Who Died."

THE SABBATH BRIDE'S TESTIMONY

The epigraph from Deuteronomy is cited in the 1985 translation published by the Jewish Publication Society: www.sefaria.org/Deuteronomy.31.20 and 21.

THE BLACK ARK VERSION

Epigraph from Robert Walser's *Fritz Kochers Aufsätze*, translation by Steve Connell; I'm not a businessman, I'm a business, man—from "Diamonds from Sierra Leone" (Barry/Benjamin/Black/Harris/Patton/Sheats/West), Dungeon Rat Music (ASCAP/EMI April Music Inc. (ASCAP)/EMI Unart Catalog Inc. (BMI)/Gnat Booty Music/BMG Monarch (ASCAP); It is what makes it possible . . . in civilized life—from Sigmund Freud, *Civilization and Its Discontents*, translated by James Strachey; This'll be the day that I die—from "American Pie" (McLean), Songs of Universal Inc. (BMI); He blew his mind out in a car—from "A Day in the Life" (Lennon/McCartney), Sony Music Publishing; How can we sing King Alpha's song in a strange land?—from "Rivers of Babylon" (Dowe/McNaughton), adapted from Psalm 137.

WHO KNOWS WHERE THE FUNK GOES?

I heard he sang a good song, I heard he had a style—from "Killing Me Softly with His Song" (Fox/Gimbel), New Thunder Music Co. (BMI)/Rodali Music (BMI); I've always kept a unicorn, and I never sing out of tune—from "Solo" (Denny), Warlock Music Ltd (PRS); Live out your fantasy here with me, just let the music set you free—from "Into the Groove" (Bray/Ciccone), Bleu Disque Music Co. Inc. (ASCAP)/Universal Polygram International Publishing (ASCAP)/WC Music Corp. (ASCAP).

OPERATION BEATNIK

John F. Kennedy's words in the epigraph are taken from his "Address at Rice University in Houston on the Nation's Space Effort," September 12, 1962, in *Public Papers of the Presidents of the United States of America: John F. Kennedy, 1962* (US Govt. Printing Office, 1963); the lines by Richard Loris Jones are from "The Moon Is Made of Gold"; "Please Mr. President" is adapted from "Please Mr. Kennedy," as performed by Justin Timberlake, Oscar Isaac, and Adam Driver in the film *Inside Llewyn Davis* (2013); this in turn was adapted from a 1960 song called "Please Mr. Custer"; Moondreams may be fascination, love can be our destination—from "Moondreams" (Petty), Wren Music Co. (BMI); C'mon people now, smile on your brother, Hey! Let's get together, try and love one another right now—from "Get Together" (Powers), Irving Music (BMI); Superman and Green Lantern ain't got nothin' on me—from "Sunshine Superman" (Leitch), Donovan Music Ltd. (PRS); As we live a life of ease, every one of us has all we need—from "Yellow Submarine" (Lennon/McCartney), Sony Music Publishing; Well you sure look good in the sky at night, and it's sad to say you won't shine so bright some day—from "Poor Moon" (Wilson), EMI Unart Catalog Inc. (BMI); Planet Earth is blue, and there's nothing I can do—from "Space Oddity" (Bowie), Essex Music.

ACKNOWLEDGMENTS

Seth Almansi, Mike Cohen, Steve Connell, Trevor A. Dawes, Darcy Lockman, Darryl McDaniels, Marty FitzPatrick, Pam Fye, Allen Goldberg, Evian Guilfoyle, Jennie Guilfoyle, Geoff Heeren, Art Hondros, Philippa Pham Hughes, Wendy Katten, John Konno, Peter Metsopoulos, Jeb Loy Nichols, Ed Park, Josh Rogin, Rob Rush, Martina Salisbury, Ryan Schneider, Anne Snouck-Hurgronje, Steve Silverman, Sharon Simpson, Nancy Stade, Stik Figa, Dan Swartz, Jasper Swartz, Mike Swartz, Robert Swartz, Deborah Wassertzug.

BIOGRAPHIES

MARK SWARTZ is the author of three novels: *Instant Karma*, *H₂O*, and *Summertime Jews*. His writing has appeared in *BOMB*, *Chicago Reader*, *Bookforum*, *Brooklyn Rail*, *Fence*, *Mississippi Review*, *New York Observer*, the *Village Voice*, and *Another Chicago Magazine*. He lives in Takoma Park, Maryland. More at www.swartzmark.com. X: @swartzmark. Spotify: OtisBlue.

JEB LOY NICHOLS is a singer-songwriter, artist, and writer. His most recent album is *The United States of the Broken Hearted*. www.jebloynichols.co.uk.